Cherish Desire Singles:

The Studio

The Complete Seven Part Series

featuring Priya

Written by

Max D

brought to you by Cherish Desire

DEDICATION

This book is dedicated to all those people always changing in the pursuit of affection.

No matter how hard you try, you will always run out of currency to pay for transactional affection. And the price of a display of caring will always increase once someone knows how precious it is for you. Free yourself to be the exotic monster you were meant to be.

CONTENTS

Erotic Themes

This book is intended for mature audiences. Cherish Desire books contain erotica adventures featuring intense sexual situations including alternative lifestyles, perverse pleasures, and supernatural lust.

"The Studio 1: Transactions (A Priya Story)" themes: FF, MF, D/s, Exhibitionism (Photo, Video), Dildo Play & Wearing, Vaginal Penetration, Implied Anal Penetration, Oral Sex, Implied Vaginal & Anal Sex

"The Studio 2: Serving Her Whims (A Priya Story)" themes: FF, D/s, Femdom, Vaginal & Oral Sex, Fingering & Implied Fisting & Double Fisting, Dildo Play & Wearing, Vaginal & Anal Penetration, Double Penetration, Gender Transition, Exhibitionism (Video)

"The Studio 3: Conquest By Choice (A Priya Story)" themes: FF, D/s, Femdom, Oral Sex, Fingering & Fisting, Dildo Play & Wearing, Vaginal & Anal Penetration, Double Penetration, Stretching, Gender Transition

"The Studio 4: A Pet By Any Other Name (A Priya Story)" themes: FF, MF, D/s, Fingering & Fisting, Implied Dildo Play & Wearing, Rubber & Latex & Fetish Wear, Gender Transition, Exhibitionism (Couples Room)

"The Studio 5: Marks Of Service (A Priya Story)" themes: FF, D/s, Femdom, Fingering & Fisting, Dildo Play & Wearing, Strap-On Sex, Vaginal Penetration, Gender Transition, Exhibitionism (Video)

"The Studio 6: The End And The Means (A Priya Story)" themes: FF, D/s, Femdom, Fingering & Fisting, Dildo Play & Wearing, Strap-On Sex, Vaginal Penetration, Gender Transition, Object Insertion (Saline Bag), Inflation Play, Stretching, Exhibitionism (Video)

"The Studio 7: The Party Favour (A Priya Story)" themes: FF, FFF, D/s, Femdom, Threesome, Fingering & Fisting, Vaginal & Anal Penetration, Oral Sex, Gender Transition, Exhibitionism (Couples Room, Photo, Public)

"The Studio 1: Transactions (A Priya Story)"

written by Max D

Featuring Priya and Max

"The Studio 1: Transactions (A Priya Story)" themes: FF, MF, D/s, Exhibitionism (Photo, Video), Dildo Play & Wearing, Vaginal Penetration, Implied Anal Penetration, Oral Sex, Implied Vaginal & Anal Sex

A Go Fund Me site seemed like a good idea. She could quickly raise some cash, move to Brighton, and set up there. The only difficulty was convincing people to contribute, but everyone was happy to see her getting to the coast. There were parties, plenty of good fun, and she had some great ideas on jobs and ways to cover her costs. It all added up to far better options than where she was.

Priya logged in again, grimaced, and fought down her anxiety. Forty quid. That's all she had raised in two weeks. Worse. She was pretty sure friends who promised to help out were just laughing at her instead. It's not like they couldn't skip a few ciders and chip in. They simply didn't care or were counting on her giving up.

That made hearing from Max even more unnerving. "Quick question," he had messaged earlier in the evening, "I need some help with memorable selfies and eye catching photos for one of my projects. Do you have anything I can license? Would you be willing to model for a photoshoot if not? I can invest one hundred and fifty pounds, but I'd need between thirty and forty images to make that worth it." It would be easy money, but it also meant risking his irritation and negativity.

Of course, she pretty much had to say "Yes" if she wanted to really move at the end of the month. She'd modeled for a few of his other projects, licensed her make-up selfies, and it wasn't difficult work to do. She probably had enough images to earn the money without even doing a photoshoot. However, that part of the offer intrigued her. Modeling - safe for work sorts of stuff only - might be another way to raise additional cash. Even though she preferred being behind the camera, it could lead to other opportunities and funding for her move.

Sipping her water, the seductress weighed her options. She could ignore the message as if she'd never seen it. She could say "Yes" to the existing photos and take the money. She could probe for more information about the photography shoot, establish the rules, and see if she could double her earnings. The easiest was to continue ignoring Max the same way he ignored her.

He was breaching their mutual détente after all. More than that. He was asking for something personal.

Priya decided to sleep on it. She knew he'd be irritated if she didn't respond, but that was his fault. It wasn't until the next evening, when she was chatting with a former Mistress, that things got put in perspective. "So what do I get... if I donate to your Go Fund Me?" Priya had been talking up the older woman in hopes of a donation that would double her total so far. "It's not a charity run after all. You're going to spend the proceeds on yourself." Her former Mistress wasn't being coy, but her support clearly had strings attached.

There were some lines Priya was careful not to cross. Solicitation was one of them. As tempting as it might sound, the seductress was very aware of how demanding paying customers could become. "Well, it would be really nice of you," she countered the unspoken sexual expectations, "but I understand if money is tight." Sometimes implying men couldn't afford something goaded them into action.

That never worked with her Mistresses. "I understand. Well, if you need help when the time comes then let me know. I could come around and help with packing." Too many broken promises had hurt her heart, and too much money had exchanged hands for the older woman to get in too deep with

Priya again. "It was nice to see you." It was also clear that the woman now considered the invite for drinks was predicated on putting a couple of twenties in Priya's pockets.

"Oh, don't go. You were going to tell me about your new pet…"

With a smile, the older woman gently raked her fingernails over the seductress' arm. "Another time. When you're more settled." The urge to invite Priya over shined brightly in her eyes, but she restrained herself. "I should have an early night anyway."

Priya left ten minutes later to avoid ending up on the same bus. She was frustrated and hurt by the understated rejection that surrounded her. She wasn't going to give up on Brighton. She wouldn't be stopped even if everyone was against her. There had to be a way.

Whether it was the drinks or her anger overcoming anxiety, she messaged Max on the way home. "One hundred-fifty for the selfies and photos I have. How much for the photoshoot, and who is the photographer? I have a lot of outfits I can model." Other men would have immediately asked for nudes, but Priya wasn't surprised when Max didn't.

"Ok. Let me know your current email address, and I'll invite you to a OneDrive folder for the current photos and send you the money once they've arrived. David can do the photography. I'd need the two of you to sort out a schedule and studio time. Two hundred-fifty plus travel expenses for you, and

I'll talk to David separately on his fees."

Go Fund Me may have failed, but Priya had basically pocketed one hundred-fifty pounds for her existing Facebook profile pictures. Even if everything else fell through, she was feeling much better when she climbed into bed. Chasing dreams required hard work and determination, and she was going to live up to the challenge.

~~~

Posing the model, camera in hand, Priya remembered that first shoot. One of only a few, despite the good pay, because of her personal inhibition and terror that any risqué photos might be used against her. David was a close friend of Max, enthusiastic and brilliant, and he had done an ace job of making her look great in multiple outfits. She wasn't as good behind the camera, but her skills were in selling what she produced. It was an interesting side business, most of the models were paid with copies of the photos unless they were in demand, and the best photos could be sold to calendars, sex stores, and cheeky card advertisers. Every model signed a release, and it was all above board. Priya didn't ever entrap or harass the ladies who modeled for her.

Most probably didn't know any better, but it wasn't her job to teach them the consequences of spreading their thighs or posing nude with suggestive toys. Her job was to find the right lighting, angles,
~~~

and poses which made the average woman a fantasy. That might require digital alterations, but Priya tried to stay true to what her eye found attractive and what the lens painted on the CCD.

"Just a little further," she coached the slender blonde. "Almost touching. Go ahead and move slowly, and I'm sure we'll get it." Long pianist fingers curled around the thick icy blue shaft of a ridged dildo, and Priya kept the shutter button down while the narrow head approached, bumped against, and then retreated from the woman's innocent looking labia. "Perfect. Lean back into the cushions... suck in your belly and push your shoulders back... Relax. Your neck is looking really tense. Ok. Ok. Good. Just lift your left leg up... bend at the knee. Set it right there. So great."

The model flashed an eager smile when praised. Her red lips were complimented by soft pink blush and hints of silver and crimson eye make-up which Priya had used to transform her from wholesome to desirable. With a few more shoots, the seductress was confident that the blonde would be pulling off wanton and lusty. She'd paced the younger woman deliberately, capturing the steady transition from the girl next door to the dirty slut at the club. Even the backdrops she was using had subtly changed from a casual living room to a posh boudoir. After every shoot, Priya promised the buyers that her model would go further but only if there was an advance deposit.

The model wasn't being paid though. She was happy posing so she could have super sexy photos for her boyfriend, and her genuine gratitude for having her travel costs to Brighton covered was proof of her sincerity. All sales from the images went to Priya, and the modeling release included digital and print rights for the seductress. A four part book including other models combined with a racy calendar set was in the works, plus a few websites were paying Priya for specific shots. It was definitely a money maker.

David had been surprisingly small and thin, despite a great bushy beard which was all the vogue those days, and his easy laugh and jokes had provided insights into better preparing a model for the photoshoot beyond makeup, lighting, and clothes. "He must really love your curves," the seductress murmured after stepping forward to fix some mussed hair. "Has he liked the studio shots?"

She knew what was coming before the blonde said anything. Men have a voracious appetite for visual affirmation of their fantasies. That's why cosmetics, lingerie, and alcohol all relied on oversexualizing women. "He..." the model was honestly blushing, and Priya was pleased to capture the moment of unfiltered hesitation as the younger woman pursed her lips and sought the courage to share her intimate secrets. "He really likes them. If we could... if you had time... then maybe we could try a bit more?"

Knowing how worked up her buyers had become after seeing the initial nudes, Priya gently encouraged the sort of thing that would allow her to cash in. "We could change things up. Shift the lighting to the platform, use some sheer muslin as a sheet to wrap you in, and…" Hesitating was part of implying she was as uncertain as her model about going forward. "What happens happens."

Trembling, the lean blonde got to her feet and gave Priya a hug. The seductress had to extend her arm to keep her camera out of the way, holding the naked woman close with a hand on her bare hip, and sighed. "I knew you'd understand. I even brought some toys if that's ok. Nothing crazy. He gets worked up so easily, but I can't take the photos by myself. They look so terrible." She backed away, worried by Priya's silence, and then caught the photographer's eye. "You always make me look so pretty."

Understanding the role she needed to play to help her model transition into soft porn photoshoots, the seductress smiled and feigned holding back her feelings. "He's a very lucky boyfriend." In real life, Priya enjoyed women as much as men, but affection and interest have different aspects than sexual desire. "I try to do my best so you'll be happy."

"I know," the blonde was wringing her hands unconsciously. "If, you could…"

Beckoning with one finger, Priya drew the woman close enough to gently kiss her lips. The tingling shock of electricity they shared made the model's knees weak, but Priya barely noticed. "Would you like me to put on some lipstick… leave a red kiss on your breast… maybe we can add a heart… for him to see?" It was important to pretend this was for the woman's boyfriend and not her personal enjoyment.

"The Studio 1: Transactions (A Priya Story)"

"I could... do that for you if you want."

Nodding bashfully, the blonde replied, "Yes... I mean that would be really cute. I'd like that. So would he... of course." She dared to kiss Priya back, was surprised by the softness of the petite woman's large breasts, and whispered, "A lipstick kiss... maybe lower... might be really sexy."

Their intimacy was not surprising. Priya had been checking the model's labia for stray hair and using foundation to even out the skin tone of her mons and pelvis over the past few shoots. Easing the model to lower her barriers, to relax her inhibitions, and to build up the courage to go further was part of Priya's job. The transition from a professional interest to personal involvement was the real prize that the seductress had aimed for all along. "Would he want to see your lips on another woman's body?" It was a gamble, but the younger woman seemed ready to make the leap. "I... might be able to help with that."

"Yes," the model sighed.

Each step along the way, the seductress used the camera as a way of maintaining professional distance. Some of the women strove to do the same, their expressions and body language emphasizing their disconnection from emotion. Cold expressions and mechanical poses were coloured, shaped, and captured in digital formats to produce the self-objectification of identity and sexuality which coddled the low self-esteem of men who were willing to pay. Other women desperately sought to bridge the divide, to prove their attractiveness and desirability, and Priya's photos chronicled their descent from angel to succubus, from casual beauty to wanton sexuality, and from wistful sensuality to lewd obscenity.

The model's moans as she writhed against the willing mouth of a masked volunteer would only be available in the video. Priya's digital shutter captured the blushing breasts heaving as her back arched, but every image was silent. The camera watched and dutifully recorded the fingers sinking into the soft flesh of her lover, the muscular line of her thighs as they flexed, and the smeared red lipstick that remained after a frenzy of kisses had smudged her makeup. The audible wetness was invisible to the lens, hidden by the long blonde hair of the guest model who did her best to inspire the arousal Priya wanted for the scene, but it would be captured in the post coitus glow. Priya already had a makeup pencil ready for drawing the heart pierced with an arrow that her paying audience knew as the model's signature iconography.

It was branding. The woman was a product. Her eyes were glowing, uninhibited sexual need visible in the contours of her pursed lips, and she focused on the camera while the tongue swirling over her clit made her tremble. She didn't need words to say it. The photographer had shown her how to express herself with just a look. Her boyfriend's attentions had become mechanical, his cock responded better to her photos than her caresses, and what remained was the attentive eye of the gorgeous woman who never turned down a request for another photoshoot. Remembering to relax, to make it look natural, she blew the camera a kiss while letting her thighs spread apart, and the rush of her heartbeat was inescapable as Priya stepped forward in anticipation of the unfiltered sexual exposure to follow.

On cue, the blonde volunteer withdrew from the heated triangle of the model's mons. Her head turned to the side, lips caressing the pale inner thigh beside her cheek, and the timing was conspicuous and practiced. Breathe. Kiss. Slip further back. Breathe. Kiss. Slip further back. Each iteration removed more of her from the frame. Each repetition exposed more of the model's swollen labia and pink clitoris. Breathe. Kiss. Slip back. Priya had trained her helper well after pointing out that her angular face might not make for the best photos, but she would do whatever was possible to create a charming digital portfolio in exchange for assistance on special studio days. Breathe. Kiss. Wet lips dragging over soft skin as the lingering scent of pussy filled her nostrils and made her dizzy. Breathe in the willing sexuality offered not to her but to the woman behind the camera. Kiss. Slip further back. Breathe. Kiss with tender affection that would never be seen or judged. Slip further back.

She never asked Priya to see the photos of the women she was asked to help with. The blonde understood the need for discretion, the way her mask hid some of her features to make her more appealing to the lens, and she preferred living in the moment over witnessing the lush beauty crafted by the seductress' digital brush. Her last kiss, placed on the side of the model's knee marked her goodbye, and the blonde handed waiting fingers the makeup pencil before slipping away to wash up. Priya's soft praise was conveyed with a smile, but her camera never deviated from the sexual display centered in its frame.

Gasping to catch her breath, the model carefully drew her mark on the pale inner curve of her pelvis. Her slender pink clit was beautifully exposed, peeking out from beneath the folded skin of her hood, and the lights leant a shiny glow to the wet trail that began at the model's exposed pearl and flowed along the lush gradient of her swollen outer labia. With her thighs spread apart, the ripe peach of her sex hung open enough to showcase the model's inner labia as well. The twisting curves of the delicate ridges were drenched in stringy saliva and thicker fluids providing proof of her arousal. Reaching down slowly so the camera could zoom in on the gesture, the model caressed and tugged her pussy open to make sure there was nothing left to the imagination. Only then, after using two fingers on each side of her wet outer labia to hold them apart, did she take a deep breath and begin rubbing her clit with deliberate swaying of her wrist.

Priya backed away, eyes glittering with pleasure, and the model's low moan conveyed her satisfaction. It had taken so many photoshoots to learn how to masturbate properly, to know what looked good, and her confidence boosted her arousal as the model tipped back her head and pushed her breasts out. Shooting scenes with dildos had been a way of distracting the audience from her unreadiness, but this climax proved that she had listened and learned how to present herself without any gimmicks. Clenching her kegels, shuddering as her thighs and abs tightened, the model's orgasm was acted out to produce the images that proved her sexual prowess. The need to concentrate, to be aware of her body and her facial expressions, added even more intensity when the moment came.

Panting, she looked to Priya for approval with a contented smile. A final photo. Priya turned off the video camera that had been watching the action as well. She set aside her camera and rewarded the model for her practice and patience. Fingers slipping over warm skin. Tongue gently probing behind soft lips. The orgasmic flush lingered as the seductress leaned close and whispered, "He'll finish so quickly..." Her hands slid down, cupping the model's wet pussy, and then tested the hidden depression of her tight bottom. "Does he like videos of anal sex?"

Shivering with need, the model succumbed to the unspoken temptations that had been guiding her all along into the photographer's control. "Yesss..." she exhaled with terror and hunger. "Oh, yesssss..." Fingertips pressed harder at her unyielding pucker, and she understood what was required. "We'll have to start with dildos all over again. We'll have to... go slow so you can show me how it's done. We'll..."

"Shhhhh..." Priya kissed to her lips. "We'll do it together. Step by step. I'll show you how to make it look so hot. So good."

~~~

With studio fees, time spent going through shoots, taking on photobooth gigs at fetish and play parties, and chasing down money owed while paying bills, Priya was keeping very busy in Brighton. Her FetLife profile and publicly accessible studio portfolio hinted at the extremely intimate results of her photography. For work reasons, Priya compartmentalized what she could and that included applying certain boundaries on Max. She wasn't exactly out of touch with him so much as they maintained their distance. Every now and again, motivated by pride or amused by the idea of tempting him, she'd share some of her recent photoshoots. He never commented.

A masked blonde looking up with innocent eyes while smooching Priya's heavy breasts. A pixie cut brunette fingering another woman's pussy while pouting with shining cherry red lips. A tall amazon punk grinding a strap-on deep into Priya's bent forward body while flashing metal horns at the camera with her free hand. Innocence lost as a demure woman rests her cheek on a monstrous dildo. She included afterimage selfies, with Priya's breasts marked with make-up and her labia loose and wet, to convey the implied sexual adventuring without context.

She'd leave that to Max's imagination. With a laugh, hitting send from the ladies toilets after a quick shag, it seemed like a good idea at the time.
~~~

"The Studio 2: Serving Her Whims (A Priya Story)"

written by Max D

Featuring Priya and Ash

"The Studio 2: Serving Her Whims (A Priya Story)" themes: FF, D/s, Femdom, Vaginal & Oral Sex, Fingering & Implied Fisting & Double Fisting, Dildo Play & Wearing, Vaginal & Anal Penetration, Double Penetration, Gender Transition, Exhibitionism (Video)

"You can see, Mistress," the naked woman murmured toward the camera while sitting on her bed, "how hard I'm trying." Her petite breasts were capped by dark nipples, and her fingers pinched and tugged on them while she blushed. "Everything..." she added softly. Her legs parted, lean thighs spread, and her shaved pussy was visibly red and swollen. "Your fuck stick is making me very sore." Despite the distraction of her nudity, the woman's nervous energy and need for approval was very obvious. "I know you asked me to..."

Priya murmured encouragement, her deep voice soothing her pet's anxiety, "At your own pace. You look so beautiful and enticing." Her slow deep breath provided a moment of calming silence. "Tell me what your goals are. For you. For all the sexy things you want to do." The caress of her praise was almost too much, but the seductress understood the intimate cost of giving in to her demands. She wanted her pet to seek out what came next, to want it, and this was a delicate moment when the balance between them would finally tip forever in her favour.

Nodding, her submissive unconsciously reached up and pushed back her long blonde hair, exaggerating the milky white curve of her neck and the natural swell of her breasts, before replying. Despite an urge to close her legs, to bring her knees together, practice had trained her well to make sure her sexuality was on display. The camera watched her entire body, unlike her Mistress' focused lens, and her coaching made all the difference when it came to expressing lust in a visual manner without succumbing to inhibition. "My goals..." she sighed happily with a contented grin. "Mistress," her comfort using that title to refer to the special woman that had taught her so much about her sexuality said a great deal, "you don't want to know my goals." The rebellious streak had come out over multiple photoshoots in Priya's studio which started with casual suggestive content and led to soft porn involving fetish costumes and masturbation. "You want to know that your big fuck stick is sliding into me, forcing my pussy open, and leaving me bruised and swollen. You want to know that two of my fingers - three when I'm in the bath - push into my bottom, and I'm working on more. You want to know..." she lowered her voice and bit her lower lip to tease the camera and her sexy domme, "that I don't need a boyfriend, keep having one night stands in toilet stalls and alleys with women, and come home with pussy juices on my face and fingers." Despite trying to seem bold and brazen, the pretty blonde couldn't hide the way she blushed from her cheeks to her cleavage. "Mistress," she took a breath, "I need more."

The seductress watched as her pet's trembling fingers stroked over her abdomen and seized her red labia. "And what do they want from you?" she whispered as the woman tugged on her bald lips.

"To fuck me. To ride my tongue." Her breasts shuddered as she gasped for breath. "To push me to my knees and pull my head under their skirts." Her middle two fingers sunk into her pink opening as her others pushed back her long labia. "They tell their friends. Tell everyone." Her palm was rocking against her clit as her legs shook, and a third finger slipped into her wet heat. "They... say..."

"What do they say, love?" Priya made it seem so casual, so normal, and that inspired spasms of desire as her pet strained to look up toward the camera despite how her back bowed forward and her pelvis was bucking against her hand.

Unable to slow down, unwilling to stop, the woman's pinkie finger joined the rest. She moaned while leaning back against a stack of pillows and pushed down with her legs while thrusting into the stillness of her living room. Pussy and fingers lifted into the air, her entire body writhed with desperate need while seeking fulfillment and satisfaction. "That I'm..." her panting whistled between her pursed lips as she struggled to enunciate the words. "I'm a lesbian slut." Even if her chest ached, even if that was only the tip of the iceberg, it was enough to send her into a spiral of hard contractions which soaked her fingers with thick girl cum as her thighs locked together over her hand.

Pleased, her Mistress replied, "Well, that doesn't sound right." Her pet was collapsing against the pillows, hand slipping from her bruised sex, and the seductress' words were shaped for maximum impact. "A lesbian slut doesn't need big fuck sticks to stretch her pussy." The blonde whimpered and spread her knees in a gesture of submission to her state of arousal. "And a lesbian slut gets fucked and sucked and fingered by her pulls, but you don't, do you?" Wet fingers leaving a slick tail on her thigh, Priya's pet raked her claws over her lean legs in a superficial attempt to distract herself from the truth of her Mistress' assertions. "So... not a lesbian slut..." she murmured with perverse glee. "Not really."

Chest aching, body on the verge of breaking down, the young blonde didn't know what to do. "Mistress?" she pleaded with that one word. "Please."

"The Studio 2: Serving Her Whims (A Priya Story)"

"Yes," Priya smiled. "How many?"

"Wha... what?" Trembling and uncertain how to answer, the submissive unconsciously looked around her room before remembering to focus on the camera in front of her. "How many?"

Unrelenting yet gentle, the seductress pushed the woman past the point of no return. "How many pussies have cum on your fingers, on your lips, on your nose and chin?" She watched with pleasure as her question rendered the blonde defenseless, unable to deny her sexual hungers, and moved on. "How big does my fuck stick feel? When you ride it? When you're on your belly pulling it into you with your hand? When you feel it slide out so easily after you cum?" The quivering reaction was impossible to miss, and Priya was certain she could actually see her pet's pussy clenching in anticipation of its next fuck. "I want you to try something for me," she didn't need to command the blonde because every lusty inspiration would find fertile soil in the woman's imagination. "I want you to start packing... to wear a special silicon cock in your pants... so you can feel how ready you are to transition."

Eyes closed, fingers limp on her pale thighs, the blonde exhaled her willingness and disbelief. "Not a lesbian. A man in a woman's body. That makes so much sense." Despite her lean build and petite size, she'd always been a rough and tumble tomboy. "But why... Your fuck sticks... I don't... understand..."

"You've never heard of a man fucking his ass for

pleasure?" Priya softly chided her pet. "Of course, you've got a better option. As long as it's rough. As long as it's hard enough to feel. As long as each time stretches you, pushes your limits, makes your pulse throb in your forehead..." The physiological response was fascinating to observe as the seductress watched her pet's body twitching and flexing as if it needed to physically mold itself to match the mental image within the blonde's mind. "That's why boyfriends were never so satisfying. You're not gay. After the first few times, they weren't giving you the rush that you've always needed from sex." Priya blew her pet a kiss to soften the blow, but the seductress knew the fixation she was implanting would leave a lasting mark that would be nearly impossible to escape. "Not a lesbian slut..." she murmured, "... my gorgeous, androgynous, sexy boy."

Broken and reforged over the anvil of her Mistress' whims, the blonde reached down and began pinching and tugging on her clit and labia. "So that's why I've always enjoyed this," she moaned happily. "Jacking off like this." Her forearm shook as she pulled hard enough to make her reddish lips turn white as they were yanked from her pelvis. "Always... afraid... of how long they might get." She was breathing hard again, the exertion and excitement roaring through her body, and the blonde groaned as the tightness across her pelvis became pain that she needed and accepted now that she saw herself differently. "Mmmmmm... Doesn't matter. No need to hold back." She swallowed, remembered to open her eyes and present herself to the camera, and reached down with her other hand so she could pull on her pussy with both sets of fingers individually gripping her stretched lips. "Will you help me pick one? Will you show me how to wear it?" Sinking deeper and deeper into the identity that Priya projected onto her, the blonde stumbled onto other fantasies. "Will you suck my cock, Mistress? Will you bend me over and fuck my ass with your strap-on? Will you-"

Cutting her off, Priya reminded the blonde, "You already wear your sexy sundresses and lace lingerie for me." It took a moment to sink in, the realization that she'd been cross-dressing for the domme all along, and her feverish blush made the seductress grin. "I might," she murmured, "deep throat your cock if it's big enough."

On the cusp of another orgasm, her pet gasped while imagining what that would require. "As big as my fuck stick," her voice shook as her eyes burned with intensity, "maybe bigger." Giving up on repeatedly pulling on her labia and clit, the blonde experimented with flattening her petite breasts to her chest while eye fucking the camera. "Will you gag on my cock while I fuck your throat, Mistress? Do I need to hold you by your ears and make sure you know what I need?" Her rebellious streak became something else, something more masculine and predatory, and when she reached down between her thighs now, it was with far more brutal intentions. "And what about your ass, Mistress? I know you finger it. I know my tongue can slide right into it. Should I bend you over, fuck you like a whore, and listen to you cum while my big cock drills into you?" The sting and wet smack of the first blow echoed in her room, but the blonde thrust her pelvis out to make it even easier to slap her pussy. "Will you help me pick a cock big enough to satisfy you? Or should I order the biggest one I can find because even that might be too small for your loose pussy?"

Thrilled by her pet's sudden aggression, Priya seduced her with possibilities the blonde hadn't even considered. "Your fists are so small though," her languid tone contrasted sharply with her submissive's angry ferocity, "so you'd need both of them to properly stuff my pussy." The thunderous battering of her pet's slapping set a rhythm for the experienced woman's taunting. "Get the biggest one, but you'll still be too small. Thankfully, you can pick and choose a cock - and they make bigger sizes than you would have had naturally. And," she smirked, "if you want to fuck me properly then those breasts better be bound and hidden. As for my ass," the low growl of her amusement made the blonde miss a stroke and smack her inner thigh, "I'll be fisting yours every time you're packing. And you'll be plugged as well. So..."

"It's only fair," the submissive pleaded.

Nodding, Priya replied, "There is no fair. If you earn it..."

Suddenly very focused and still, her pet asked, "How?" She wasn't sure what her Mistress wanted, but her damning desires had already taken root.

"You will be the best boy for me. Do you

understand?" The blonde slowly shook her head, anticipating that she wasn't aware of what that could mean, and waited for clarification. "You will be packing, plugged, and properly bound. And..."

"Yes, of course. And?"

It all came down to this. The entire setup and staging which made this proposition acceptable after overcoming each barrier and boundary the blonde had placed in Priya's way. "Since you will be packing, since you want to fuck women so much..." Her pet nodded in full agreement. "It doesn't matter how stretched and loose and open your pussy is, does it?"

Swallowing as she felt out her emotions, the submissive realized her Mistress had a good point. "Not at all, Mistress." If she would be wearing a cock under her clothes, if she was a man enjoying every woman that let her have a taste or go with them, then her sexuality wasn't defined by her pussy at all. It made sense after all. She'd been pulling acquaintances, using drunken excuses for sexing up women she knew as well as strangers, and none of them even offered to caress or finger her sex.

"When you show me you mean that... then I'll pick out the right cock for you to wear while fucking my bottom."

Hope was all that her pet needed. "I will. I totally will." She reached down and shoved four fingers into her sore sex. "Will that turn you on? Seeing how hard I'll fuck my holes? Knowing it doesn't matter to me anymore?" Shove was the appropriate verb. It emphasized her commitment to so much more. Access to her Mistress' sexy ass was simply a token of her intentions. "Should I put my cock in a cage for you as well? Will you enjoy reaching under my skirts and stroking my shaft?" Her hunger inspired so many dirty fantasies. "Will I be..."

"My boyfriend?" Priya finished the question for her submissive. "You'll need a big cock to convince me."

"One for your throat and one for your cunt," the blonde sighed. "Definitely." Her knuckles were grinding against her labia, but she couldn't get any deeper. "And the one you choose for your ass."

Thrilled by how easily the transition was going, Priya was careful not to overplay her hand. "And the cocks that you'll be packing. Big enough for the bulge to show in jeans. They'll look huge when you're wearing leggings." The seductress' soft moan tortured her pet. "Rolling onto my belly," she whispered, "and taking my vibe out from under my pillow."

"I know what you want to see," in shock but confident that her Mistress could be woo'd and won over. "Let me show you."

Holding her breath while tickling her clit with the soft silicon pad of her Cuddle vibe, Priya watched as her pet's long hair cascaded forward toward the camera. Everything was a blur, and then the image stabilized as the sexy blonde repositioned herself with an icy blue dildo between her thighs. "Yes," Priya encouraged her as she watched the pointed glans fit between the woman's swollen labia. "All the way."

The last barrier between the seductress and her intentions collapsed as the blonde pulled the sex toy all the way into her pussy without any hesitation. As the last couple of inches penetrated her, when the Kelvin's knot thickened to just over two inches wide, her arm shook from the force required to drive the silicon into her sex. "I know this is your special fuck stick, Mistress," she smiled at the camera, pulled on the broad base until she was sure the dildo wouldn't fall out, and then played with her nipples while suggestively bucking her pelvis and hips with the cock embedded in her pussy. "I could see the teeth marks." It was short, only six inches of articulated shaft, and that had made it easy to notice the subtle notching all the way down to the bulge of the knot. "It must have felt so good fucking your throat."

"Better with your juices on it," the seductress took a deep breath and then let it out as the warmth within her sex slowly spread into her belly. "So much better."

Swallowing as she rose to the challenge, the blonde murmured, "Is that how you like it? My cock soaked in pussy juices that wet your chin and lips as I press it into your mouth?" She thought about the teeth marks, wondered how many times her sexy Mistress had gagged on the Bad Dragon dildo, and closed her eyes. "This cock specifically. Straight from my pussy." She could picture herself the way the camera would see it. The way her Mistress would show her. "Except it will fall out so easily. Slide in all the way. The right size to stuff into your throat... but so small otherwise." Her eyes were bright when they flickered open. "It's too small for you, too," she realized with a gasp. Her lurid fantasies escalated with a sudden frenzy. "You let me have it... you..."

"Your fist will be too small, too," Priya growled happily. "And you needed to know... to feel it... to be ready."

"To be knotted." Shivering as she realized what was really holding the bestial dildo in place, the blonde nodded her acceptance. "Whatever you want. However you want it. You know I only enjoy it when the stretching and force fucking pushes me over the top."

"Because you prefer fucking women," her sultry pleasure was accompanied with labored breathing as her vibe triggered an early climax. "You prefer licking them, fucking them, and..." A brief gasp was followed by deep breaths before the seductress could finish her thought, "... and leaving them loose and swollen and bruised from your big cock."

Intimately connected to that sensation, knowing how it had thrilled her to steadily work up to her Mistress' thick fuck stick, the blonde couldn't deny her preferences. "I love seeing it. I love how it feels with my fingers. I love..." She sought out her clit, wedging her fingertips between the base of the Kelvin dildo and her pelvis, and shuddered when her fingernail snagged on her tender flesh. "I love it rough," she squirmed as the unanticipated pain encouraged her. "I..."

The seductress filled in the blanks, subtly seizing control of her pet's fantasies, and provided the vocabulary the blonde didn't have. "You told me about your first time. How good the hurting felt. How sexy being bruised and sore was. He was too fast after that, didn't fight your clenching long enough, and you knew that you needed more." She could see her submissive slowly rotating her hips, the broad base of the icy blue dildo blatant between her pale thighs, and the uncertain pleasure from being knotted and awkwardly stroking her clit needed a focus. Priya gave it one. "How many boyfriends before you came to my studio? A dozen. Maybe more. How many one night stands? Excited by the rush of adrenaline but disappointed by the same old action. You didn't know then. You couldn't see yourself the way I do. So I showed you. Looking through my lens. Watching yourself. The woman you were fucking all along because you've never been effeminate like her." Her pet was nodding, mesmerized while basking in the sensations of the female body she was thrusting into, and the passing emotions that ebbed and flowed across her countenance gave a sense of conjoined duality separating into distinct identities with different motivations. "You liked me telling you the truth. Teaching you how to fuck her, how to stretch her, and how to make her cum even when she was scared and didn't want to. You liked seeing her perform for you, masturbate for you, and do exactly as she was told. You wanted more though. You were confident enough to try it on your own, to pull a one night stand, and to lick her until she orgasmed on your chin. You don't even know, can't even remember, how many women you've sucked and fingered." Legs trembling, the blonde was clearly playing back the collision of innumerable nights out spent stalking sexy ladies. "Like any man, it was all about the conquest. Did you even take time to notice which ones had plush labia versus long thin lips? I'm sure you could tell which ones were tighter, but you used as many fingers would fit without asking if they preferred only one. You knelt between their legs in the toilet stall, slipped your fingers under their dress in a dark alley, and did whatever it took to get into their pussies." She soothed her prey with gentle sounds despite the harshness of her judgment. "It better fall right out next time I see you fuck my special throat cock. I want you to watch your videos; I want you to tell me how you're going to fuck her; and you will do whatever it takes to make sure she has a pussy that turns me on. Juicy. Stretched. Gaping. Bruised. Big enough to handle two cocks at once. Loose enough to need both my fists. So hollow that she knows the only way to get off is an enormous fuck stick." Shifting tones while the blonde was still in a self-induced sexual trance, Priya set out the steps for her progression. "I expect you at the studio tomorrow for one last shoot before you begin packing your cock daily. I'll provide you with what you need to get started. Your next shoot after that you will be dressed properly as a man who loves fucking pussy should be."

"You know I do," the blonde murmured.

"And a grown man can handle keeping his bottom plugged. Especially if he expects anal from his girlfriend."

Still deep within her sexual euphoria, the blonde's buttocks clenched in anticipation. "Whenever he wants anal. Always. He always wants it so he'll always need to be plugged." Her body writhed while leaning back into her pillows.

"I'm not the jealous sort," Priya teased her transitioning submissive, "so you can have all the pussy that you can get, if..."

"What, Mistress? What do I need to do?" Her sincerity was so perverse that the seductress turned on her vibe again to enjoy it purring beside her clit while watching the blonde completely give in to her soft spoken demands.

"You know exactly what you need to do. To every one of those pussies. To each and every one of those tight quims."

Beads of perspiration alluded to the sudden hot flash that surged within the submissive's bare body. "As many fingers as I can. More. Using my tongue to tease them, to coax them to keep going, and making them cum while I stretch them open." So close but unable to climax, the blonde resorted to bargaining for the inspiration she needed. "Tell me how. Tell me what to do. I'll fuck every one that I pull. They think I'm a lesbian slut. Worse. They think I'm desperate and in the closet. They'll make fun of me, but I'll know which ones are already riding three fingers. No matter what they say, they'll want it when they are drunk enough. Is that enough? Mistress? What more should I be doing?"

"Are you disappointed when you watch the videos?" It was such a cruel thing to say, but what was coming next required provoking her pet's sadism. "So much potential. So sexy but inhibited. Didn't you want to bend her over? Wouldn't you force her to keep going? Doesn't she know it's for her own good?" While her submissive wildly bucked her hips while trying desperately to go beyond having her pussy stuffed with the silicon dildo, Priya murmured, "Give her a choice, of course. If she can't handle another finger thrust in alongside the cock in her cunt then maybe two in her ass will be enough. To start with anyway."

"At least two," the blonde gasped. She tried, fighting to fit her fingertips alongside the thick knot, but it wasn't going to happen. So she reached behind her back, stroked over her tailbone, and began pushing against both her tight pucker and the lump of the curved knot inside of her pelvis. "She'll need to get used to it anyway," Priya's pet bit down angrily while her arm shook from the deliberate force applied to her bottom. "There. Two to start with, but I'll use three later." Her partial satisfaction and deliberate escalation wasn't lost on her Mistress. "And if it's not easier then I'll knot her ass until four fingers slide right in."

"The Studio 2: Serving Her Whims (A Priya Story)"

Pleased by the evidence of disassociation, the seductress purred, "She'll probably like that. Having her ass busted open. It's not like she'll say no to a hard fucking." Her submissive's grimace evoked an evil chuckle. "Oh, perfect. Three already. She'll learn to take it."

Seething with irrational fury, the blonde responded, "She will. She will fucking take my whole damn fist. I'm not going to be disappointed any longer." Licking her lips while lewdly fingering her ass alongside the hard bulging knot within her pussy, the submissive's aggressive alter ego blossomed. "All of them. My hands are so small. Training size. They'll cum so hard without even knowing."

"Will they even be able to enjoy cocks again?" Priya loved the sudden shadows of dark rage that distorted her pet's features. "Only your big fuck stick..."

"Bigger than this. This is only big enough to fuck a bitch's throat. My big fuck stick will make this look tiny." Her body bucked hard, and the blonde had a hard time catching her breath. "There. Four fingers." She looked hungrily into the camera. "What will it take, Mistress? To truly fuck you? I should have asked the first time I kissed your lips."

"Do you really want to know?"

"I'll prove it. You know I will. Tell me."

Secretly amused by her submissive's demands, the

domme played coy and uncertain. "What if it's too much for you to handle? What if you don't like my answer?" She had her pet eating out of the palm of her hand.

"I know it'll have to be thick and long. I know you need it. Tell me and I'll..."

"You'll what?"

Seizing upon the obvious from the perspective of her aggressive male ego, the blonde replied, "Not only her cunt. I'll fuck her ass until it's a loose hole, too. You want to see that. Want to record it for your private collection. That's how you get off... just like I do. Watching sluts learn to fuck for you." It was almost too close to home, and Priya didn't dare breathe. "Make sure the studio has plenty of things for her to fuck. I won't let her stop. I won't let her cry. She's going to perform for both of us."

"Ace," Priya replied and sealed the deal with a smile. "My biggest fuck stick is three inches wide at the top and gets all the way to the four inch thick mark eight inches down the shaft." She made her request clear. "I want to go further, but I need to know I have a hardcore slut to turn me on while I break my cunt. You provide that, and I'll let you be the one to strap on my fuck stick and hammer it into me."

No further negotiation necessary, the blonde replied, "Done." Her crumpled fingers slipped from her ass, and she leaned onto one thigh while sitting. The icy blue silicon base still hid most of her shaved pelvis. "I didn't cum."

Shrugging her Mistress replied, "It's not my job to help boys wank off. Why don't you watch some of those videos and let me know what got you hard? Or, better, watch those videos and tell me what our bitch needs to fuck in the studio to make you splurt?" She laughed and waved even though there was no way to see her. "Maybe knotting her ass will help you sleep better."

The last few seconds of video captured the shift in posture and transition from one identity to the other. The blonde was in tears, quietly begging and pleading for patience, but there was no one there except herself. She didn't try to deny what needed to be done; only asked for more time to prepare and work up to it. When that all failed, she got up and turned off the camera before going to her bathroom to clean up. The trickles of fresh blood from the tears within her rosebud and vaginal opening required rinsing off in a hot shower before it was time to lube up her bottom and do her best with the Bad Dragon dildo.

"The Studio 3: Conquest By Choice (A Priya Story)"

written by Max D

Featuring Priya and Ash

"The Studio 3: Conquest By Choice (A Priya Story)" themes: FF, D/s, Femdom, Oral Sex, Fingering & Fisting, Dildo Play & Wearing, Vaginal & Anal Penetration, Double Penetration, Stretching, Gender Transition

Her eyes pleaded with the mocking glint in the curvy woman's glare as the words cut deep into her heart. "Oh, so now you want some? Thirsty much?" All the blonde could do while a small clique of women at the pub judged her was try to hold her ground and nod. Her chin quivered with anticipation and humiliation when the object of her lust pressed two pudgy fingers against her lips. "That won't do. Go ahead. Suck them like you mean it."

The inviting red of her tongue dabbed over the

whorls of the larger woman's fingertips as soon as her mouth opened, dancing around the manicured nails and coaxing the fingers deeper, and the lean blonde blushed crimson red as she performed for a leering audience. The pressure increased until the woman's second knuckle slipped past her lips, flattening her tongue until it couldn't move, and cruel laughter made her chest ache as the woman withdrew her hand enough to make a blatant thrusting motion while bobbing her fingers in and out of the glossy lipstick edged hole.

"Much better. You're such a slut." The insult was intended to be a hard slap to the lean woman's face, but she never stopped licking and sucking on the fingers. "Well," the curvy woman sighed and shared a knowing look with her friends, "I need to go to the loo." She deliberately hooked her fingers to seize the blonde's cheek and drag her in tow. "Be back when I'm satisfied."

Roaring laughter and cheering followed them as the sashay of hips was followed by the obedient blonde's eager tottering as she was tugged along. It wasn't until they were in the stall, door closed behind them, that she whispered, "You know I would never tell them."

Pale thighs shook as they clenched together, but the blonde's four fingers were already thrust deep within the trembling woman's sex. She'd been reluctant at first, insistent that a single finger was all she ever used by herself, but her wet arousal betrayed her fading pretense of innocence.

"You..." she gasped. "You wouldn't dare." Her only choice was to humiliate the blonde, to destroy her credibility in advance, because if any of her so-called friends really knew...

Leaning forward to press into the generous bounty of the woman's breasts before kissing her lips and exploring the lingering bitterness of gin and tonic on her tongue, the blonde's arm was trapped between them. Every damning motion of her fingers flexed between their abdomens. Every whimpering gasp was preceded by the nudging motion of her elbow. Every deep breath was interrupted by the tapping of her wrist against the woman's pelvis. The resistance was intense, a battle of wills, but the blonde's insistence won out.

Stumbling backward until her back was pressed against the water pipe running to the tank overhead, the larger woman's legs parted as her pussy clenched with orgasmic spasms on the fist bobbing within her sex. "That's what I thought," the blonde whispered coyly. "You love it." Thick juices clung to her wrist as her knuckles teased tender pleasure triggers within the pulsating grip of the curvy woman's lust. "Will you lick my hand clean?" She winked with a sexy grin. "Lick it clean with me, I mean."

"Fuck..."

The blonde cut her off with a firm kiss that plunged her tongue into the other woman's mouth. "Yes," she growled in a soft alto, "fuck." She tugged her hand downward, the base of her palm and thumb joint pulling the woman's pussy outward, and then grinned as her hand was sucked right back into the warm hollow that immediately held it tightly in place. "You don't have to tell them," her lips murmured as she stole the ragged exhalations of the panting woman, "but I can always come over to your flat if you need me, too."

"I can't... No..."

With a dramatic sigh, the blonde pulled back as if she was done and going to return to her outward display of obedience and diminishment. There was visible relief on the other woman's face, her skirt still bunched up around her waist and the feverish perspiration of her lust leaving her cheeks glistening pink, but the blonde stole that moment of reprieve from the other woman's grasp with a sly smirk. "Get one of those big tits out," her soft command seemed to echo in the toilet stall. "I want to see your teeth marks all over your nipple and soft udder when I finish."

She didn't wait for a response before squatting down and thrusting her forehead into the gathered folds of cloth to make room for her tongue to seek out the woman's clit. As soon as she had found her way to her target, the blonde was entirely focused on her intentions. Even after the fast orgasm induced by penetration, she knew that lingering need and desire required far more direct attention.

Shaking, trying to control the blonde between her thighs by seizing her head, the curvy woman shook while battling with her sexual hungers. There was no one to see, no one to judge, but she unconsciously defined the difference between herself and the blonde hungrily lapping at her sex in terms of self-restraint. She wouldn't be ordered around. She wouldn't be humiliated by her lust. She wouldn't be told what to do.

Warm breath tickling the soft curls of pubic hair that served as an unintentional barrier between the outside world and the larger woman's sexuality, the blonde projected her voice enough so the muffled words could be heard. "I think," she spread the generous folds of the woman's labia with her other fingers while probing deeper with her fist, "that another two fingers will fit." Her delighted grin couldn't be seen as she used a single questing digit to slip alongside her wrist and pry open the slick furrow of the other woman's sex.

Then she stopped, held completely still, and waited.

Shuddering so hard that her knees might buckle and legs collapse, the hands on the blonde's head were withdrawn with a deep groan. She held onto the wall behind her, trying to support herself while reeling from shock, and then her hands reached into the deep V neck of her blouse, and tugged one melon sized breast free. "I'm... Just two more.." she whimpered with a hoarse rumble. "I'll..."

The second and then a third finger went in. "You'll have a key made for me." The blonde covered up her duplicity by tucking the extra digit close to her hand while actively stretching her prey

"The Studio 3: Conquest By Choice (A Priya Story)"

open with her knuckles popping against the taut elastic band of the woman's opening. "Did you know?" Her tongue darted over the woman's sensitive clit, nose buried in the humid heat trapped beneath the curvy woman's skirt, and dared to try sneaking in a fourth finger along the others. "How sexy you'd look shaved?"

Tugging her breast to her mouth, the larger woman almost missed the words. As soon as her teeth grazed her soft milky white skin, she felt the deep pressure of the blonde's fist rotating slightly within her abdomen. It ached and then blossomed and then erupted with intensity as involuntary clenching suddenly collapsed her entire sex to a single frantic fiery point somewhere slightly above her clit and behind her navel. Her inner thighs were drenched with squirt juices as the immense orgasm tore through her with the same force as a malevolent thunderstorm.

They both fell backward. The blonde ending up on her ass with her back against the stall door. The heavyset woman slumping to the toilet in a dazed shock. It took long minutes for them to find their way back to the social subterfuge the curvy woman needed to make her submission and sexual stimulation acceptable.

"Well, you're going to need to clean up all this mess." Her haughty tones might have had more force of conviction if she hadn't been fighting to catch her breath. "I hope your tongue is up for it because I'm not getting paper towels for you again."

Fully aware of the squirt and girl juices all over her face, arms, and chest, the blonde nodded submissively and looked toward the floor. "But you did like it?" She was the picture of guilt and low self-esteem. "I mean... You wouldn't mind if I came over?"

Huffing while digging into a pouch hooked onto her belt, unaware of how undone she looked with slobber on her exposed breast and skirt circling her waist while a pool of juices seeping from her pussy gathered on the toilet lid between her thighs, the curvy woman gave the illusion of seizing control of the situation. "I'll add your number to my phone. A good slut's tongue shouldn't go to waste." She waited and then punched in the digits when the blonde recited them to her. "You're such a mess. I bet you're too tired to even care."

Ducking to one side, the blonde didn't protest as the curvy woman stood up on unsteady legs, adjusted, and then swept out of the stall. She was hit by the door when it swung inward, and the object of her desire had to slide sideways to get out. She heard the cheering and applause and laughter that greeted her conquest, even when the door swung shut again, but it had been worth it. She licked her fingers clean, disappointed that she didn't get a chance to smear the thick juices all over the other woman's face but looking forward to another opportunity, and then took out her own phone.

"A fist and four fingers," she texted to her Mistress. "She came so hard and then she came again and squirted."

The response was too quick to be spontaneous. The blonde's phone slowly displayed a picture of creamy thighs with glistening fingers covering the soft triangle of her Mistress' shaved pussy. "Rolling onto my belly," the seductress replied coyly. "My ass feels so wet tonight."

Chest filling with pride and lust, she sought more praise. "Her number. So I can fuck her at home as well." There was no response, so the blonde tried again. "My ass has been plugged all night, too."

"Mine as well." Her Mistress devastated the lean blonde with those simple three words. "If only my boyfriend had been here instead of stretching pussies at the local pub..."

Two competing emotions tore her apart. At first, she was pleading, typing "Please... I'll come right over..." but she angrily deleted all of that before hitting send. Unconsciously grinding her bottom against the hard floor, forcing the plug in her bottom to press deep within her ass until her tailbone was crushing the silicon base, the blonde replied, "If your ass was ready for my fist then you should have told me." Aggression was translated into sharp stabbing motions of lean fingers as she dared to taunt her Mistress for teasing her. "I'll need a bigger fuck stick for your loose cunt anyway. Maybe I'll bring a bottle home with me."

Priya's response evoked memories of her hand lazily dragging over the smooth glass of her smartphone while enjoying the perverse pleasures that warmed her libido. "Both. My big fuck stick made me cum so hard, and now I'll be so wet and loose even with this plug in my ass." The words had time to inspire wicked visions of the eager seductress masturbating before she continued. "I've got my gloves right by the pillow. For when you come over. For when I bend you over. Don't disappoint me."

"You know I won't."

"You already are."

Growling as she forced herself to her feet, the blonde all but shouted at her phone, "You better still have your cunt and ass stuffed when I get there. Leaving now." She only took the time to push her clothes around to be decent, and then stormed out of the stall, past the gaggle of women waiting to humiliate her, and out through the crowded pub. "I want that ass so slippery that I fall right in."

Priya's moans were understood even if she didn't text them. "I'm not as stretched and fucked as you. Your big fuck stick will hurt so much."

"You think your fist in my ass is comfortable? Lube that hole up or I'll tear it open." She checked on the bus times and started walking. If it came along before she arrived then it might take a few minutes off the journey. Otherwise it was twenty minutes on foot to Priya's flat. "And get that vibe on your clit, slut. You need another cum, don't you?"

"Ass plugged. Fuck stick in my wet cunt. Vibe on my clit." The seductress was making the blonde blush while dominating her through acts of submission. "What else should I do before you get here?"

"Only your plug? You know you need something bigger to spread your ass."

"Yes. Your big cock is right next to my thigh. Waiting." There was a long pause and then another message. "The head... already fits... Two cocks inside of me."

Raging while trying to ignore the shin splints interfering with walking any faster, the blonde replied, "Get that dick up your ass, slut! Do I have to be there to shove it in? And why isn't anything gagging your throat?" Her arousal was literally running down her legs, raising goosebumps as the cool night air stole the warmth from her exposed skin, and there was no denying the throbbing of her pulse in her forehead.

"Leaning back. Riding both cocks. Grinding against each other. Going deeper." Each motion was its own universe of sensations. The seductress left that to the blonde's imagination. "Deeper than the plug. Burning and wet. Vibe on my clit. Clenching so tight. On my belly again."

"Your fist and two fingers," the blonde dared to risk giving more in her state of eager frenzy. "Deeper."

"Your fuck sticks are so big." The blonde stared at her phone, waiting for more as she stormed across a dark intersection, and was rewarded by the time she reached the opposite curb. "Sliding in. Even further. Stretching my cunt so well."

"You bet it does." Her body actually hurt in anticipation, and it was impossible to take a deep breath. Five more blocks uphill, then a left to plunge down a street of endless row houses, and her Mistress waiting almost at the end. A night bus roared by, but it was going the wrong direction. "All the way in."

"I won't feel cocks for weeks," her Mistress complained.

"Mine should be good enough!"

There was a long pause, the blonde's labored breathing echoing within the quiet, and then her Mistress answered, "A fist and two fingers." She tried to shake it off, but the tightness in her belly overwhelmed her focus. "Pulling my gloves on." Broken, the blonde tripped over her own foot and almost dropped her phone before catching herself. "I hope you wore your biggest plug tonight."

Aching for the tainted pleasures of her Mistress' flesh, she choked back a sob while texting, "You're done already?" If she had missed the action, if all she was doing was delivering herself to be painfully fisted, then maybe she should stop or even slink back to the pub.

"I want to fist your tight ass while enjoying how well your big fuck sticks are stretching me." An audible gasp was accompanied by the renewed drumming of the blonde's feet on the asphalt sidewalk. "You know how loose I'll be when you pull them out."

"And replace them with my fist."

"Charging my vibe. I'll need it while you fuck me so hard."

Every minute after that was an eternity and a blur. The world couldn't turn fast enough, her feet couldn't carry her steadily enough, to get to her Mistress' bed. The last handful of blocks were agony as her shins, calves, and thighs finally rebelled. Forced to take halting steps, hurting with each inch closer to her Mistress' perverse pleasures, the blonde was nearly undone and in tears when she got a final text message.

"Door is unlocked. I expect you naked, in my room, in the next ten minutes."

Breaking into a run, the blonde painfully raced down the uneven sidewalk to service her Mistress' needs. It never occurred to her to resist, to hold back, or to demand more. As she crossed the threshold, carefully locking the door behind her while simultaneously kicking off her shoes, there was no doubt this was the decision she had made.

It fit in with never wearing panties. Always wearing skirts knowing it made her exposed bottom and sex accessible. Keeping a plug in her ass and a smaller or larger one in her sling bag in case she needed to adjust at some point during the day or evening. Applying lube regularly to keep her labia frosted and slightly glistening, and knowing to apply more when she could no longer feel the chilling tickle of fresh air caressing her wet lips. Riding the big dildos her Mistress gifted to her each night. Sharing her sexual exploits with the seductress who always wanted to know the humiliating and lascivious details of her corruption and her prey. Encouraging and enabling their perverse fantasies with offers of more frequent and greater acts of arousal and lust.

Clothes in an untidy pile by her shoes, the blonde went up the stairs into the darkened boudoir of her Mistress' lair. The wet fingers slipping over her mouth, scented with slick pussy juices, took control of her and guided her to the bed. Bent forward by fingers pressing into her shoulders, gliding over her bare skin, she celebrated the familiarity and intensity of her connection to her Mistress. A gloved hand, smooth latex coated in thick greasy lube, explored the gap between her buttocks. Leaving a mess from her tailbone to her thighs, several initial tugs failed to grip the wide plug firmly enough to remove it. The fingers on her lower back drifted downward, caressing the curves of her left cheek, and then seized the silicon and yanked it from her clenching pucker. The sudden shock of removal was answered with a demanding thrust of the well lubed gloved hand directly into her hole.

At first, only the blonde broke the silence within the dark room. "Your fist and two fingers." It was meant to be a reminder as well as a promise. She was only rewarded based on the pleasures her body was willing to provide.

The smooth fingers went deeper, knuckles disguised by the thick latex, and her bottom was pried open. The steady flow of her Mistress' intentions battered against her resistance until there was a long pause.

"So lubed that I'm a sloppy mess," the blonde murmured. She shivered when her Mistress pulled back, but her request was fulfilled with a palmful of vaseline ground into her trembling pucker. "It'll take days to rinse away." Her voice was so soft that the sudden rush of fingers into her ass seemed louder by far.

The transition from four fingers to four and a thumb was breathtakingly obvious. The blonde wondered how her prey at the pub could have overlooked the change in shape and pressure necessary to wedge all but the top of her hand into her sex. Of course, the distraction of pleasure, the post-coital glow of a fierce unexpected orgasm, and the alcohol helped. Her Mistress gave her clarity instead. Deliberate, intentional, and direct, the seductress rocked her hand between the parting curves of the blonde's buttocks while working her way deeper and deeper.

"I will have a bigger plug for you in the morning." It was an understated command that hinted at disappointment. "This will not be acceptable in the future."

Swallowing, willing her body to relax while knowing she couldn't control the way her inner walls clenched down on her Mistress' fingers, the blonde nodded. "As big as your fist. Of course." She was unhappy as well. If she couldn't satisfy the passions of the seductress then she might not get her chance to wallow in the depravity that inspired her hungers.

Priya ignored her. Focused on the necessary act of contorting her fist, crushing her hand into a tight ball and then stretching her fingers deep into the raging heat while trying to exhaust the muscles inhibiting her, and the thick jelly lube melted and ran down the pale thighs of the woman bent over the bed. For a moment, the clenching stopped, and a hollow sucked her deeper. Then the woman's ass clamped shut and squeezed down with a viselike grip.

"I'm trying," the blonde whispered. She was discouraged, fully aware of her failing, and uncertain what to do next.

The answering growl soaked her pussy in an instant. "You make it very clear," the seductress forced her hand closed into an iron hard fist while pushing forward with her entire body, "that her cunt will be as ripped open as your ass." The raw fury ignited the embers burning within her ass, and both women shook as repeated heaving thrusts began breach the tight passage's opening. "Bigger than my fist."

Aching, there was barely a hint of disorientation as two voices responded in her head. The feminine one pleaded for more time, for another chance, and to go slow. Booming masculine laughter drown that out while savouring the pain and adrenaline as the seductress demanded her payment in full. "Whenever I want to fuck your ass." His machismo was aggressive and brazen. "And that's all the time."

Slick fingers teased the swollen labia below her wrist, milking the passionate turmoil within her pet, and Priya murmured, "Your fuck stick feels so good right now. So tight. Wedged up my ass alongside your cock in my cunt." She was almost knocked backward by the eager bucking motion that encouraged her fist to go deeper. "You know how much I need it. When I feel like this. When only a big cock will satisfy me."

Reaching back, yanking on her buttocks to spread her ass open, the blonde replied, "Your fist and two fingers. Did you lube your fuck holes enough? Are they as slick as my ass? Will my fist slide right into you, slut?" She felt the tearing as the girth of her Mistress' palm and thumb joint were driven past her opening. "If you were stronger then you could punch fist my ass. Fuck it the way you really want to. Maybe we should work out together."

"The only workout you want involves me on my belly," the seductress murmured. She knew every word was recorded and loved the way her submissive pet readily embraced dangerous hungers. "My fist," she pressed deep enough to make room and then dug into the taut pucker surrounding her wrist, "and two fingers."

Suddenly orgasming without any physical buildup, the blonde collapsed forward and breathlessly demanded, "Your turn." She didn't grasp how much influence her Mistress exerted over her, and she didn't care. When the gloved fist and fingers remained in her bottom, brutally preventing her clenching grip from squeezing them out, she added, "Or three fingers if you want."

"Whenever I want," Priya confirmed. "This is how I prefer to fuck you, but you're ruining it for me."

Accepting the irritation of her Mistress, her response was far too easy to give and much harder to practice. "I'll fuck my ass every day. Wear a huge plug. Whatever it takes to make sure you can enjoy fisting me."

"If I let you fuck my ass?"

"I..." She hesitated. The trap was so obvious, but she'd almost walked right into it. "You'll have what you enjoy," the blonde replied instead of risking turning their intimate frenzies into boring sexual transactions.

A blown kiss tickled her ears and the seductress murmured, "Good. Because I'm going to enjoy you so much..." Leaning forward, heavy breasts resting on her pet's back, Priya gently asked, "Are you my cheating boyfriend? Did I smell pussy on your lips?"

Moaning as the hand in her bottom subtly rocked in place, the lean woman exhaled the words with tender care. "I'm here now, aren't I? You know how horny I get." The two fingers alongside the fist in her ass slipped away and petted her sex. "Whenever you call, I'm here for you. You don't want me nosing around like a lost puppy, do you?"

She didn't know enough about her Mistress to understand the laughter her comment provoked. "Here for me... would mean ready for my fist. You know what I need? Why do you make it so hard?" Another aspect of Priya's life was surfacing which the blonde knew nothing about. "Is it so difficult to be good for me? For me first?"

That last barb stung, and they both took a deep breath while letting it settle. Her pet responded as best she could, united in wanting to please her Mistress, and the words were so sincere that they broke the woman's heart. "I want to be everything you need me to be." She swallowed, breathing in, and almost wishing that dragged the words back into her chest.

"Me, too," Priya sighed happily. "Just making sure."

"The Studio 4: A Pet By Any Other Name (A Priya Story)"

written by Max D

Featuring Priya and Ash

"The Studio 4: A Pet By Any Other Name (A Priya Story)"
themes: FF, MF, D/s, Fingering & Fisting, Implied Dildo Play & Wearing, Rubber & Latex & Fetish Wear, Gender Transition, Exhibitionism (Couples Room)

He was slender with long blonde hair and an effeminate face that made him seem Elvish. The tightly cinched latex corset wrapped around his torso and enforced good posture while exaggerating how his pale complexion contrasted with his deep plum outfit. The matching trousers were baggy in the crotch and thighs but fit snug around his calves before plunging into polished black boots. The extra room was needed for reasons emphasized by the snaking curve of a very thick shaft protruding from his pelvis and slipping down his inner thigh. It terminated in a clementine sized glans halfway to his knee, and it didn't matter if the people who looked and stared believed it was real or an accessory.

The outline of an enormous cock got his message across.

His Mistress, a curvy seductress who only came up to his shoulder, was happily chatting up a few ladies nearby while he waited at the bar. Slender pianist fingers cradled coins for another Stella, and the bartender hid his surprise when the blonde man ordered with a sweet feminine voice. Served his pint, the slender man wandered closer to his flushed domme after paying for the beer.

"You know," she was flirting with a doe eyed brunette whose robust cleavage had almost entirely escaped her top, "you'd be amazed at the things you will do for the taste of something you truly desire." It didn't matter if the banter was sexual. The group of women were following along in eager anticipation of hints of perverse pleasure. "It doesn't matter what it is. It won't matter who knows." She leaned in close and whispered a command to the younger woman's ear no one else could hear before returning to her casually confident monologue. "Oh, I think I need to go dance to this song," she winked at the blushing target of her wicked suggestion before turning and gesturing to her pet.

They walked away, not saying a word, but that didn't stop the words from forming in his head. His Mistress didn't need to check to know his ass was plugged. Dangling from her elastic wristband were her keys and a small black remote control. Once they were on the dance floor, Priya put it to good use - nudging the buttons to a setting she felt suited the music - and watched her companion adjust as a rhythmic cycle of small electrical discharges evoked cycles of clenching with his unseen abs and partially hidden buttocks.

"Feel good?" she teased while shuffling close enough to rock her breasts against his flat corset. "Miss me?" the seductress blew a kiss while reaching under her asymmetric latex skirt. "Need a taste? A reminder?" Her pussy juices wet her companion's lips as he tried to disguise how eagerly he inhaled the scent of the lewd woman's lust. "You'd do anything for more, wouldn't you?"

His voice was the one thing that never changed. "You know I do," he answered, but the words were sung in the sweet tones of a woman whom he fucked every night. "What more? What would you like?" His hungry eyes searched his sexy Mistress' body for a hint or a sign of her desires. The latex clad crowd and stage performances were reduced to background noise as he narrowly focused on his chances of driving his cock into her throat, her pussy, or her ass. Preferably all three if she was willing. Without thinking about it, he lifted his pint and tried to quench his thirst with Stella, but they both knew he needed something far more potent and profound.

"I want," her fingers dragged over his latex hip as Priya stepped forward and straddled his thigh and cock, "to hear her howl like a banshee in the couples room while you fist her pretty hole." The doe eyed brunette, uncertain but trying to be brave, was approaching them from the steps near the bar. "Do you understand?"

"Only couples," he murmured in his high pitched voice while nuzzling her forehead.

The seductress laughed. "Oh, I have my own little slut to attend to. Find me in there. Bring her with you. Sit as close as you can." She blew him another kiss, this one far more suggestive as it brushed his lips, and smiled. "Don't forget the lube and latex gloves in your hip pocket."

When she tottered off, pausing to hug the pretty brunette, the blonde man was left waiting for the fawn to step into their trap. It was no surprise when the younger woman rushed forward, not meaning to appear so needy but wanting to close the distance before her courage failed her, and he let her give him a hug. They danced together, his fingers caressing her cheeks as he complimented her busty top and multi-coloured latex skirt, and it wasn't long before he popped the question. "Would you like to go someplace quiet? Someplace where I can listen to your heartbeat under my palm? Someplace away from this crowd?" She was already nodding, fighting the urge to tug on his hand, and he sighed. "The couples room won't be private though. There will be people... doing things... you know..."

"I want to," she squeaked. Gritting her teeth in frustration over sounding so foolish, the brunette repeated herself with more confidence. "I want to. Let's go." She turned to pull him along, but he held her back. "What?" she asked looking over her shoulder.

"She told you, didn't she?" Slumping and looking embarrassed, he let the young woman come close and hug him again. "I... She noticed I fancy you. I was too afraid to say anything."

Kissing his bare shoulder, pleasantly surprised by his supple strength, the doe eyed brunette whispered, "She told me you wanted to play. With me." Her teeth grazed his pale skin, and he hummed appreciatively. "Let's go. Come play. With me." His vulnerability was so easy to understand. He probably didn't even know what to do. The pleasure of seeking out another lusty soul and unleashing it from the bondage and restraints of inhibition inspired her arousal. Her imagination began with a hug and a kiss and carried them all the way to the couples room where they were invited in and found a quiet corner to begin the petting and fondling that she always looked forward to but rarely got lucky enough to enjoy.

He knew better, of course. As her delicate fingers stroked his thick cock through his latex trousers, he caressed her throat. "Leather," the blonde whispered before nipping her ear lobe. "But you wouldn't want to wear my collar..."

Surprised and excited by his subtle dominance, the doe eyed woman licked her lips before kissing him. "I would," she rubbed her nose against his. "For special occasions." Her boundaries weren't really defined, and she was happy to make exceptions suited to the fantasies he might enjoy. "Do you-"

"Want a taste?" the blonde man's tongue danced with hers for a moment, and then he leaned back and took a deep breath. "Can you handle that? Is it too much to ask?"

"Oh, god... what?" She could already see him between her thighs, and she didn't know why it felt so wrong and sexy at the same time. "Could I handle what?"

Guiding her fingers, gently pushing the smooth latex up her thigh, both their hands slipped into the shadows under her skirt. "Just a taste," his eyes never left hers despite how their fingers were fumbling over the curve of her inner thigh. "It'd be too much..."

He met resistance - her latex panties barring his way - and she gasped. "Fuck," she exhaled before probing the curve of her pelvis and seeking a way past her own defenses. "No. It's not too much. I'm so hot." She tugged on the latex, but it wouldn't yield. "Oh, god... I want this so much."

Holding back, letting her do the work, he gently bit her cheek and commanded her, "Take them off.

Stand up, and I'll make sure no one can see. We both need it so much. A taste. Maybe more. Whatever you can handle. Whatever you want." She was already getting to her feet, trying to understand how to discretely tug off her rubber underwear without lifting her skirt to her waist, and his hands slipped into the darkness. "I'll help." He turned as if he was covering her from being ogled by other people in the couples room, but it was a farce. Priya was less than five feet away, a pretty boy licking her pussy with her thighs holding his head in place, and the blonde made sure his Mistress had a perfect view.

Together, they wrestled with the snug fitting latex and pulled it from her generous hips. He encouraged her to finger her own sex, but they ended up doing that together as well. When he slowly licked his fingertip, visibly savouring her sweet juices while darting his pink tongue over his porcelain skin, she was completely undone. "Another taste?" the brunette offered without even sitting down beside him.

"Can I tell you a secret?" his feminine voice distracted her from his aggressive motivations. He waited until she leaned close, spreading her legs to straddle his thighs while he slipped his hands under her skirt again, and there was no denying the flushed heat of her response as he told her what he wanted while painting her clit with slick juices from her own quim. "I want to fuck you so much."

The brunette knew it, could feel the heat of their union already building up, and moaned while whispering, "But how?" Even if they could do it, even if no one would stop them, she wasn't brave enough to be so exposed in a semi-public place.

"I'll use my fingers," he promised with kisses to her cleavage. "I don't want you to be embarrassed." His eyes were pleading with her, begging for her approval as she looked down at him, and she gently stroked his hair while spreading her feet further apart. "It's ok?"

Nodding happily, she murmured, "You'll have to catch me when I cum... and... we can share a taste." Leaving him hanging with a dirty secret was enough to encourage his fingers to massage and milk her ripening labia and sensitive clit. "You're so good at this," she hissed softly.

"I want you to cum. I get off on knowing... on enjoying... how wet you get and how hard you orgasm." He guided her with subtle nudges of his elbows and forearms until she was comfortably holding onto his bare shoulders while gasping for breath. "You're so sexy... so soaking wet... so," he kissed her belly, whispering the words but knowing they carried to her ears, "ready to be fucked."

"Oh, god... I know." She really did. It was almost too much and too easy to give in. "Don't stop. That's... I can feel how much you want it... Go slow... I'm warming up still." His fingers were starting to slip into her pussy and tug on her opening. Maybe two from each hand. It was hard to tell, but the stretching was intense and arousing. He slipped out, petted and tugged on her flushed mons, and then only one hand slipped into place with four fingers - definitely four she thought - fit into her opening. "Oh, god... so much... I must be so wet..."

It didn't matter if she was or not. He had discretely palmed a pack of lube in his left hand, and, after squeezing it out over his fingers, he had rubbed it into her pussy until her well oiled labia easily slipped back and forth with his probing caresses. Now his knuckles were fitting into her narrow opening, and he bobbed his fingers in and out while stroking her clit to sustain her arousal and distract her from what he was doing. "Wet and hot," he murmured. "Is it too much? Not enough?" He tipped back his head and smiled while deftly manipulating her tender flesh. "Do you need me to tell you more?"

She nodded and closed her eyes. The sounds of other couples murmuring, moaning, and skin sliding over skin teased her ears, but his feminine voice was all that mattered.

"I'm so hard," he serenaded her, "and aching for release. You know my Mistress won't let me though. So only you get to cum... only you get to orgasm... and I need that so bad because it's everything and all I'm allowed." Thrusting slightly deeper, her opening was being strained by the girth of his fingers. "My big cock wouldn't even fit in your tight pussy," he sighed, "so I guess we'll taste you on my fingers and not my dick." Her fluttering vaginal walls gave him a way to navigate her fantasies even if she didn't realize it. "Oh, you know she does. Her strap-on... She loves to make me choke and gag on it." Her excitement

"The Studio 4: A Pet By Any Other Name (A Priya Story)"

tingled around his four fingers. A wave of clenching exhausted her muscles, and his thrusts began to go even deeper. "Should I stop? Do you even want to know any of this?"

"Tell me," she demanded while gazing down at the pretty blonde man. She felt it - trembling while the storm gathered within her abdomen - and his hints and partial confessions were more than enough to set her off. His submission was so much more than she could have imagined.

"You don't want to know," he moaned while cradling her clit and rocking it back and forth within its thin sheathe of skin. "She... keeps me plugged because she knows how much I love plunging into her bottom. She makes me do things... keep my cock in a steel cage... and go to work like that. She won't let me cum for days." He pulled back, shaking his head, and sighed. "I don't want to hurt you... You're so small..."

Seizing control while imagining herself in a position of authority, the doe eyed brunette growled, "Did I say you could stop?" His fingers dutifully resumed petting and stroking her sex, but he didn't go any further than that. "I want to feel those fingers in my pussy," her whispered roar unleashed a fresh flood of arousal as she took control. Wherever his Mistress was, she wasn't there to tell him what to do or not do. Cupping his chin, forcing him to strain his neck to look up at her, she dared to imagine punishing him while breaking out into a feverish sweat. "You don't deserve to cum."

Shaking as the knuckles at the top of his hand began rocking against her pelvis bone, he nodded obediently. "I know. Only a taste. Only if you cum." The pulsing electrodes within his body changed rhythm, sustained discharges made his buttocks and lower abdominal muscles clench for so long that it hurt to breathe, and he knew his Mistress was pleased by his progress. "It'll be easier if you're not standing... if we make you comfortable..."

She let him guide her onto her back, resting on conveniently placed cushions, and the brunette almost ordered him to tongue her pussy before remembering she wanted to taste her juices straight from his fingers. Thumb slowly stroking over her clit, his fingers fit into her with ease, and she let her legs splay out to the sides while welcoming his filling touch. There was a moment of intense concentration, when he closed his eyes and seemed enraptured, but it was the overly full feeling which seized her and triggered bucking spasms of arousal that ached all the way into her chest and thighs.

"Oh, god... You were right." Whether it was the change in position or knowing he would do as she demanded, her orgasmic wave immersed the easy thrusts of his fingers while he continued to gently nudge her clitoris and sustain the tingling that echoed all the way to her toes. He didn't stop though. As her pussy relaxed, he became more confident, sliding in and out and triggering secondary climaxes that stole her breath.

Wheezing, her low moans grew in volume as her pink pearl was milked by his slender fingers. She had no way of knowing that he was wrist deep with his closed fist rocking against the underside of her diaphragm. In the throes of a recurring orgasm, she lacked the prior experiences necessary to process how having her pussy fisted while anesthetizing lube dulled the throbbing pain of being so stretched and full was something that changed everything about the kind of penetration she needed. As soon as she could gulp down cool air, it was forced from her lungs again in short bursts of whimpered pleasure. He kept fisting her, backing away to cautiously circle but not touch her clit, until she wasn't capable of squeezing down on his hand. Her orgasms were a sweet conquest, but the increasingly easy embrace of his entire fist within her sex was what his Mistress desired.

Satisfied and true to his promise to only seek a taste, he gently eased her into an upright sitting position with his mostly dry hand before stroking wet fingers over her lips. He partook as well, knowing the lube would make his tongue tingle before going slightly numb, but he was waiting for her mind to catch up with reality. It was there after a long silence, eyes frantically scanning the room before zooming in on his soaked hand, and then looking at him in shock. "I want your number," he used his wet fingertips to pry on her lips and part her teeth before slipping three fingers into her mouth and caressing her tongue. "Fist fucking you was amazing." He let his fingers linger for a moment longer, stifling any initial objection she may have had, before removing them and licking them clean as she stared at him in horror.

"Oh, god..." It was apparently her default phrase when nothing else came to mind.

He nodded. "Or I can give you mine. So you can decide." She shook her head, uncertain and confused, and he smiled. "Decide if you really need it. If it's worth whatever you have to do to get it." He leaned in close, kissed her with sloppy wet lips, and murmured, "I was a woman before my Mistress told me what I'd have to do to be her boyfriend. You'll see. You'll understand." He took out a card from his pocket, careful not to spoil it with his slick fingers, and tucked it into her overflowing cleavage. "And my cock is bigger than my fist... but you have to earn that. Only the first taste is free."

He got up, helped the doe eyed woman to her feet, and waited patiently as she tugged her latex panties back up as best she could. No one overtly stared at her, but she felt their eyes studying her body as she went by. Not knowing what to say, what to do, she was completely unprepared for walking into the seductress' embrace right outside the couples room entrance.

"I told you he would make you cum," Priya gleefully kissed the younger woman's cheek. "Would you like to dance with us for the rest of the night?"

It wasn't clear that the brunette had any other choice.

"The Studio 5: Marks Of Service (A Priya Story)"

written by Max D

Featuring Priya and Ash

"The Studio 5: Marks Of Service (A Priya Story)" themes: FF, D/s, Femdom, Fingering & Fisting, Dildo Play & Wearing, Strap-On Sex, Vaginal Penetration, Gender Transition, Exhibitionism (Video)

"Show me," the domme commanded while reclining in her studio chair.

The blonde moved slowly, uncomfortable without the masculine accessories that suited her dominant personality, and tugged her sundress over her head. In the pervasive diffused light of the photoshoot dais, there was nothing hidden. Her long legs were well formed and muscular, her abs and petite breasts were snug and tight to her torso, and her arms were well proportioned and fit. None of that mattered though Priya demanded her pet maintain her physique.

Spreading her feet, reaching down to fluff her long labia, the attractive woman knew her Mistress' entire focus was on the contour and presentation of her pussy.

Unlike the rest of her body, her sex was distorted and swollen. Two pairs of thick metal rings huddled in close to her pelvis with long pale curtains of skin hanging between them and her inner thighs. Her inner labia resembled generous orange slices with the wedge's narrow edge aimed down toward her feet, but they didn't touch in the center. The aggressive gap was increasingly exposed and obvious as her inner thighs ceased pressing her swollen lips together. Bruises and discolourations hinted at intense saline injection sessions and other ways her Mistress had sought to enlarge, deform, and reshape the feminine curves of her pet's sex into something more brutish and masculine.

Her pet had done the same on her own even without her Mistress commanding her to do so. Trying to ground herself, the lean blonde murmured, "I've been fucking her twice as hard the last few weeks. She needed it." It seemed entirely acceptable to refer to her female body as separate and distinct from her masculine ego. "Is there a reason why you wanted to see, Mistress?"

Amused by how the heavy metal rings helped round out the impression that her submissive's sex was simply a functional feature of her pelvis, the seductress smiled and nodded. "I have questions that require answers," she replied. "Does she like it when you fuck her ass?"

Shrugging and adopting the casual indifference of the average lad in a pub, the blonde woman answered, "She doesn't complain about it. Besides, her ass needs a good pounding whenever I've got time to give it to her." There was no physical reaction - no attempt to clench or cover up - despite the very intimate nature of the question.

"And how do you like my strap-on hammering your bottom?"

The segregation of identity was so complete that mutually exclusive possibilities were rampant when referring to her body's experiences. "You like to push my limits... push them hard even. I can't complain, Mistress. You know why I let you fuck my ass and face whenever you want."

Wagging a finger at her brazen pet, Priya knew exactly what she was alluding to. "Because you know keeping me happy means you get to enjoy fucking me." She held up her hand, silencing any initial response, and drove her point home. "Is that the only reason? You'll be obedient and a good boy as long as I let you fuck me now and again? What does she think about that? Is that how she feels about you?"

Cloudy emotions cast shadows within her eyes, but the naked woman knew the right answer. "You know how skilled I am at making you feel good, Mistress. I enjoy doing that. Whatever it takes." Hand gesturing as if toward an unseen third person nearby, she continued, "And honestly, she's got nothing to say about it.”

“I’m glad to hear that because what comes next will be very hard for her,” the domme’s experiment had gone far better than she could have hoped for. Several very eclectic buyers wanted a lot more of the same results, and her pet had been an exemplary product to put her on the map for porn focused on gender transition and transformation. It was a rapidly growing market after all. “It is strange seeing you without your cock though. Could you put it on so we can talk about my expectations without that distraction?”

Relieved to hear she wasn’t in trouble, the blonde excused herself to affix her enormous soft silicon dildo to her piercings. The weight of its long shaft and scrotum was enough to constantly pull on the rings looped through her inner labia. Using body adhesive to affix her stretched outer labia to the base and sides of the sex toy had helped reshape the pout of her pussy opening. When Priya’s pet returned, the foot long shaft was also supported by a leather strap wrapping around her right thigh so it couldn’t flop around between her legs while she was walking. “Thank you, Mistress. This is much more comfortable.” She had debated putting in her plug, but it seemed better to only do as she had been told.

Again, the photoshoot set left nothing concealed. Multiple cameras were watching, silently recording, and the domme was fully aware that she’d make money off of the footage in part or whole. “She’s allowed you to ruin her cunt, hasn’t she?” Her submissive nodded. “Good. I reviewed your progress as well as your reports on working several women up to fisting. I... need something more extreme from her. If she can handle it."

"Not like I'm going to give her a choice. What would you enjoy, Mistress?"

Encouraged by the lack of self-doubt, Priya replied, "We're going to pump her up until she looks very pregnant and completely hollow out her pelvis." Her evil grin was matched by her pet's perverse ear to ear smile. "We'll start with her pussy, but..."

"Fuck. That sounds crazy hot. How do we do it?"

"Oversized IV bags, capable of holding two liters each, inserted and then filled with lukewarm water." The domme watched her pet's cock shudder with arousal and wondered if copious juices were gathering behind the base of the packing dildo. "She's very slender so even two liters by itself will definitely show a belly bump."

"And then we'll add more to really stretch her out. Wish I'd thought of that." The blonde was completely immersed in her masculine self and sported a wicked grin as she collaborated with her Mistress. "Working her up to double fisting has been hard. I was going to ask if you had any ideas on bigger fuck sticks to keep popping her cherry."

Nodding, Priya lured her pet into a cage defined by the woman's need for the rush and intensity of continually pushing her body to its limits. "She'll be very hollow, but her pelvis is still so narrow at the opening." Her pet's frown emphasized their mutual disappointment. "The bones may spread if she carries the water for long periods of time. It's worth trying. First, we'll need accurate measurements..."

The blonde didn't hesitate to make her suggestion. "What about a plaster cast of her sex? That way we get the full measure of her opening and its limits in three dimensions." It was an intriguing idea which Priya easily acknowledged with a smile. Encouraged, the woman absentmindedly stroked her long silicon cock and added, "Will you enjoy her stretch marks?"

"So much better than just bruises, don't you think?" Toying with her pet while enjoying the footage which would faithfully record how the lean woman seductively rocked her pelvis with suppressed desire, the domme tested the submissive's limits. "Does she even appreciate our hard work ruining her? What has she done to earn her marks of service?"

Chuckling, the blonde leaned back into her chair and deliberately caressed the base of her cock. Fingertips circling the top two metal piercings, stroking the stretched skin adhering to the silicon, she teased her body while demanding the trembling obedience of her feminine alter ego. "She's learning," Priya's pet replied with a sadistic grin. "A good fucking every day helps, but to really break her pussy means she doesn't get a say in it anymore." Wiping her fingertips off on her thighs, the blonde lewdly thrust upward with her cock even though the length was held back by the strap holding it to her leg.

"Four… five… maybe six hard and fast knottings when I'm in the mood. Some nights I fuck her until I'm done, nap off the rush, and fuck her as soon as I wake up again." Shrugging with a wink, the blonde clarified, "It's not like any of my cocks ever go limp, and that gorgeous throat fuck stick you loaned me definitely falls right back out. The knot is way too small to stay in now."

Thrilled by the malevolence her pet applied to her own feminine body, Priya had to take a calming breath to slow her racing heartbeat. "And?" she asked while hoping for more details.

"She's a total size queen now. Needs it. Wants it. Fucks it with tears in her eyes because she wants even bigger cocks inside of her." Enjoying how her words mesmerized her Mistress, the blonde used one hand to slowly jack off her enormous silicon dildo. "Once she's hollowed out, I don't think there's any way she could ever stop her urges, Mistress. She'd be totally dependent on us to keep her fucked." Priya was visibly writhing in her seat, and the blonde was inspired by how her words made the beautiful domme so hungry and eager. "However you want. As often as you desire."

Soaking wet, Priya used her datapad to end the session for paying customers right then. The storage cameras would continue recording, but the streaming feed was over. "You want to fuck me so much," the seductress intoned with her rich tenor, "and I'll let you… on one condition."

Pleased, the submissive unstrapped her shaft. The massive foot long silicon dildo bowed toward her calves as it hung from her shaved pelvis. "Name it." She was brazen and bold, knowing her Mistress needed more than a quick fuck, and how that gave her an advantage.

Getting up, undoing her snug wraparound skirt, the domme's eyes were locked on the big cock's shaft. "I want your ass, too." The blonde didn't flinch, but she should have. "I want to see how ruined she is with her thighs spread and cunt hanging open..."

"And how destroyed my ass is every time you bend me over," her pet finished the thought while ogling the glistening triangle between Priya's thighs. "Yes. Of course." She meant to look away, to look up, but every step closer made her dominant lover's swollen arousal more obvious. "As often as you want. I've never stopped you." The creamy thighs slipping back and forth were mesmerizing. The bald lips cradled in their intimate embrace were sufficient motivation for almost anything.

Priya stepped between her pet's knees, further spreading her legs apart, and caressed the blonde's cheeks. "I mean ruined," she whispered with exhilarating effect. The younger woman shuddered in anticipation. "Do you enjoy it? Seeing her gaping pussy. Does she turn you on?" Her fingertips slipped over the blonde's lips, and her pet eagerly kissed them. "If I was her... standing right in front of you... would you lick her... suck her... finger her... fist fuck her..." The domme loved how each word provoked her submissive. "You've been keeping count?"

"You know I have," her broken pet moaned. "I text you every night I go out." It was true. Every evening spent in the pub, usually half of it spent in the ladies stalls fingering and licking other women to orgasm, was followed by a confession of her lust and slutty pursuit of sweet feminine nectar. "What more could I-"

"Shhhhh," the domme quieted her darling pet. "What will they say when they think she's been knocked up?" Terror was quickly replaced by sadistic joy as emotions raced across her submissive's face. "When her belly is obviously bulging as you wet your face with their creamy pussy juices?" Priya firmly took hold of the other woman's chin, forced her to look up, and blew the blonde a kiss. "I want stretch marks we can feel with our fingers. Stripes that make it clear how ruined she is. I don't think anything else will turn me on."

The weight of her Mistress' arousal was a deciding factor which cleaved the blonde into the divergent gender egos that co-existed within one body. "Prove it," the masculine growl was unmistakably tainted by her feminine voice. Reaching down and lifting up her thick silicon cock, the blonde coaxed Priya to mount its thick glans. "How hard will you fuck while knowing you can stroke your hands over her abdomen and feel how ruined she is?"

Happy to oblige, Priya moved so she could straddle her pet's thigh. The broad glans was driven at her pussy opening while the domme pressed down, and they both exhaled hard when it popped into Priya's sex. "You want to... don't you?" Priya rested her hands on the submissive's shoulders while grinding and rocking against the dildo. Keeping the silicon trapped between her pelvis and her pet's leg, the seductress enjoyed the flowing girth of the shaft while teasing her clit with the smooth length.

Damned by her self-awareness, the blonde tried to deny her scheming and plotting. "Only if you do. Only what you ask me to." It was all for naught. Her Mistress was far too aware of the dark fantasies which inspired the submissive's lust. Fingers scraped over her cheek and scalp as a reminder to be honest. "Yes," she whispered, half expecting to be punished, "I wish I could ruin your pussy, too."

"My cunt," Priya corrected her, "and my ass." She kissed the younger woman's forehead. "I know you do. Maybe... maybe someday..." Hope would give the seductress even more leverage to transform and shape her pet. "After you prove to me that you've earned it."

The dramatic change was caught by the unblinking cameras as the blonde slumped forward and began to whimper. "Please. Please, Priya. I don't. I can't." It was rare that the feminine ego surfaced, but something the domme had said forced her to speak out in her own defense. "I'll do anything but... please..."

"Be gentle?" the domme kissed to the bridge of her submissive's nose. "No. That doesn't make you cum." Tears wet her lips as Priya bent down and nuzzled her pet's cheeks. "Is being mine too much? I thought you liked it."

Tipping her head back to capture soft caresses from her Mistress' tender mouth, the blonde moaned. "I do. Too much. I can't... stop liking it... even when it scares me so much." Their tongues met, tangled, and Priya explored the shape of her submissive's words with her lust. "We'll do anything for you. She'll do... She won't ever stop... fucking me for you." Her anguish dripped from her lips as the domme savoured the succulent taste of her pet's corruption.

"You will do as you are told," Priya murmured to the blonde's ear. "You are our fucking slut, and we're going to knock you up so everyone can see the proof." Her harsh words contrasted with the sweet lullaby cadence and pitch used to deliver them. "Or should I start gagging you so you remember your place?"

In the momentary silence that followed, the blonde looked at her reflection in Priya's eyes. She imagined it, felt it already, the ball gag forced into her mouth, making her jaw ache, and desperately trying to breathe around the slightly industrial taste of the rubber ball. A tear ran down her cheek, accompanied by an understanding that her imagined experience suited her so well, and she took a deep breath while embracing her fate.

"You should be." Her dominant masculine

personality roared with triumph, relishing the deep-seated feelings of humiliation drenched with sexual need, and the blonde let her head droop forward. "My..." she moaned while realizing how much her confession turned her on. "My cunt and ass. My big swollen belly so everyone can believe what they want." It was right there, at the tip of her tongue, and the blonde had no idea how her next words captured in her Mistress' video recordings would impact so many other women. "This all started because I wanted to make my boyfriend notice me." She looked up, chin trembling, and whispered, "I didn't know how much I needed this instead."

Obliging her pet with an aggressive kiss, Priya made sure to provide the praise necessary to remind the woman what was expected next. "I have a gag right over there. You're going to look so wonderful wearing it." Her lips tickled the blonde's ear lobe, and the seductress exhaled her siren's song with deliberate intensity. "It takes nine months to deliver to term."

"The Studio 6: The End And The Means (A Priya Story)"

written by Max D

Featuring Priya and Ash

"The Studio 6: The End And The Means (A Priya Story)" *themes:* FF, D/s, Femdom, Fingering & Fisting, Dildo Play & Wearing, Strap-On Sex, Vaginal Penetration, Gender Transition, Object Insertion (Saline Bag), Inflation Play, Stretching, Exhibitionism (Video)

Whimpering, the blonde clawed at the navy blue sheets while writhing on the mattress. Two finger-width nozzles protruded from her bruised and battered labia and broken pucker, and the attached clear tubing flexed and flowed with the motion of her legs and hips. "Ooooh..." her hands suddenly reached for her belly when the tubes stiffened, "it's... rushing in... now..."

Her Mistress' deep voice murmured, "Say thank you." Every time a live watcher paid a fiver, another fraction of a litre of fluid was pumped into the plastic saline sacks inside of her pet's pussy and bottom. The writing continued with a half gasped thanks, and Priya added, "Maybe today we'll see if you can handle four litres," enjoying how emphasizing the size of the audience made her pet blush. "Or maybe," she smirked when the blonde let out a strangled cry, "we have a few big buyers." A fifty pound payment triggered a surge of shuddering as the pump kept going until nearly two litres had been added.

"Thank you," her submissive pet murmured. Her belly was starting to swell, pushed outward by the filling fluid sacks within her pussy and ass, and the unsynchronized flexing of her arms and legs emphasized the slow normalization of the physical stress.

Sighing contentedly, Priya ran her fingers over the pretty woman's bare thigh. "More than halfway," she seduced the unseen audience with the lust in her voice, "and still so empty." Her pet pointed her toes, tried to spread her feet further apart, and thrust outward when fingertips danced over the smoothly shaved contours of her loose labia. "Maybe they don't understand what it takes to ruin a slut like you?" The cruelty of her words tore at the naked woman's ears, but her nipples stiffened, and the signs of arousal were impossible to ignore. "Maybe they don't understand what you fuck just to prove you're good enough to share my bed?"

The pump whirred to life, this time provoking a

seething breathless howl of triumph, and a wicked smile swept over the blonde's face. "Thank you," she was clawing at the sheets again, "for helping ruin... my cunt and ass." There was a reflexive moment of hesitation, a pause before the admission of being the woman on the table and not the visualization of the man forcing her to submit, but then her grin grew impossibly wide and tugged on the eyes as the blonde leaned back and relaxed. "I'm sure I could take at least three litres, Mistress."

"Nearly there." The clear tubing was limp and curled along the inside of the blonde's thigh, but the initial rush of fluid was evident from the elongated melon sized bulge beneath her pet's navel. "Maybe we should go further." Her hand caressed the swollen mass, circling it while exploring its dimensions, and nodded. "Every litre after the first four will cost twice as much."

"Ooof..." the blonde gasped when both tubes suddenly straightened from the pressure of fresh fluid rushing in. "Why..." her pet moaned while her legs kicked with involuntary spasms.

"Because the last liter was half off." Priya teased her submissive's protruding clit, stroking and gently capturing the pink nub with her fingertips, and then made a suggestive wanking notion with her hand. "Does it matter? You know what it takes to satisfy me."

Shallow breathing became panting as the blonde's self-control began to break. She tried sinking into the mattress, tried digging her fingers so deep that she could pull herself below the surface, but instead her shuddering body seemed to be drifting above everything. The saline bags continued to fill, unrelenting pressure crushing her bladder and pulling on her lungs from within her body, and her features were twisted with sadistic joy in one moment and terrified submission the next only to swap back again as storms of emotions shattered her calm. Not being able to see the counter, Priya's pet was denied any information that might have distracted and soothed her. Though it was unlikely knowing that all six litres were now paid for would have achieved anything beyond resignation to her fate. The pump did its work, machinery unemotional and objective, and the hydraulic penetration forcefully hollowed out her pelvis and demanded even her organs to accept her Mistress' dominance.

"Much better," the seductress sang with sincere pleasure while highlighting the enormous bump distorting her pet's abdomen. "If my cock was this big..." she teased her audience with hints of irrational sexual optimism. "Now we wait to see if anyone wants a show. Let's see how badly you want to cum even though it'll hurt so much while being stuffed like this." Priya's hands slipped away, a lingering light slap on her pet's swollen labia drawing eyes to the split peach of her lover's sex, and returned with a palm shaped vibrator. "Of course, you're going to feel this all the way into your chest."

With slick juices beginning to flow past the hint of clear plastic between her parted lips, her pet struggled to let her Mistress do as she wanted. Perspiration gathered in her cleavage and along her inner thighs. Her forearms flexed in anticipation of being overwhelmed. She could barely breathe knowing what was coming would make her scream with agony and need. "Thank you," she pleaded as soon as the vibe began humming in Priya's hand. "Thank you, Mistress." She was desperate.

For good reason. Fingers drummed against her unfurling labia with mechanical pulses of vibration that tingled within the submissive's spine. As soon as the vibe made contact with her clit, the fluid filled sacks within her pussy and ass throbbed with the same frequency. She pissed herself, unable to prevent her bladder from releasing when the drumming intensity battered her internal organs, and her Mistress' amused chuckle made it clear even that involuntary defense was not enough to prove her defeat. Instead, her clitoris was steadily milked, the pleasure a continuous reminder of the increasing pain with every attempted contraction of her distended abdomen, and the blonde was damned, devastated, and delivered directly to hell.

Pulsating waves of rigid flexing were interrupted by outbursts of flailing as the unseen audience enjoyed how Priya slowly tortured the blonde. It was obvious that they were seeing raw emotion, unfiltered by conscious awareness, and expressed through physiology untainted by any sense of self-restraint. More money came in, the pump straining against the resistance of the limits of the blonde's abdominal cavity, as it tried to add another two litres of fluid.

Then money kept coming in anyway, despite there being no apparent reward, while Priya continued to shatter her submissive's mind while enslaving her body to a repeating cycle of whimpering climaxes and frenzied drops.

Without a word while highlighting her mastery over the other woman's sexuality and need, Priya watched the clock. At the thirty minute mark, she turned off the vibe and began to seductively massage her pet's naked body while anointing her in excessive amounts of mineral oil. At the forty-five minute mark, her submissive was slick and glistening on the blue sheets, and Priya withdrew her hands with the final minute spent cupping and kneading the of blonde's breasts. At the one hour mark, she murmured, "She'll be so empty when I drain the fluid. She'll force herself onto my big cock so hard."

Petite hands placed an enormous bestial silicon dildo beside the blonde's thigh. Dark red and silver corded muscles bulged down the line of the shaft; the glans was the size of a large man's fist with no taper; it towered above the blonde's pale thigh and seemed close to the same girth as her calves. For the viewers, the money counter reset.

The exhausted submissive exhaled "Thank you" as her crumpled fingers nudged the unnatural cock's broad base. "Please, Mistress. I need it so much."

The first payments started to come in as the pump was disconnected. Splattering streams of fluid could be heard filling a bucket in the background while the blonde submissive grabbed at her abdomen and sobbed with pain. Her thorough fucking would be just as calculated, the upcoming hour luring a fresh audience with slightly different fetishes, and the best would be saved for when only private viewers with specific invitations watched how Priya slid onto the sheets belly first and enjoyed receiving the thrusts of a smaller strap-on while rewarding her pet's adoration and achievements.

~~~

Curled up on her sofa, the blonde murmured quietly to her Mistress. "It's been hours," her masculine arrogance expressed her pleasure, "and the entire flat smells of cocoa butter." The recurring sessions with the seductress rapidly flooding saline bags within her pussy and ass to provoke intense stretching had been complimented by evenings spent carrying four litres of fluid within her pelvis to reshape the hollow space within her lower abdomen. "You can feel the difference, even when she's empty, and it lasts longer and longer each week."

"Good," Priya responded with a smile that could be heard. "This past weekend..." she sighed happily. "When my fingertips stroked over her stripes... That was so sexy."

Encouraged by her domme's open praise, the blonde offered her own. "Your gaping cunt hanging wide open after my big cock fucked you..." Her voice trembled with lust, shuddered with need, and her
~~~

obsession was so obvious. "Fuck."

"Rolling onto my belly," the seductress replied while assuming her favourite position to masturbate. "You're the biggest fuck stick I've ever had in my cunt." Her words were a low whisper, the growling of her Cuddle vibe nearly drowning them out, and Priya gasped while exploring her labia and clit. "You left me so bruised and open."

"Ha," her pet barked. "A loose slut like you... you know how much your cunt needs to be fucked and stretched." Grinning while imagining obscene pleasures, the blonde teased her Mistress. "Go ahead. Cum for me. I know you can feel it. How hollow your cunt is even though it's been days since I tore you open. I know you want it. Love it. Need it." Her callous taunting provoked whimpering affirmations from the petite domme. "Every orgasm leaves you so wet... so loose... and you have your fuck sticks right under your pillow." Shaking from the intensity of her arousal, unable to ignore the ache triggered by her abdominal muscles trying to clench down on the heavy water filled bags within her sex, the blonde pushed each of her Mistress' buttons knowing that inspired further cruel demands of her own body. "If I keep them in, keep my baby bump stretching and hollowing out my pelvis, then will you lube your ass for my huge cock? Do you want to feel my big belly pressing into your lower back as I pound into your loose holes? Will you cum harder reaching back and feeling how you knocked me up?"

Moaning with pleasure, Priya's low tenor serenaded the masculine lust of her submissive's passions. "You promised... When your ass is ruined... When both my fists can fit..." Her voice broke with the rapid descent into her tumultuous arousal, and she climaxed suddenly while panting to catch her breath.

"Test me," the blonde growled savagely. "You think my big cock isn't fucking her ass, too?" She chuckled malevolently. "Yours is next."

"I know it is," Priya murmured in the afterglow of her orgasm. "I think you need to start carrying six litres from now on, don't you?" Her pet couldn't back down, and the seductress had no intentions of providing an easy way out of their spiraling demands on one another. "And if you were really pounding her ass with that giant cock of yours, wouldn't it be turning her inside out?"

"Oh, it will," the blonde promised with a grin. "It's not like she's going to stop me."

Satisfied and comfortable in her bed, Priya ended the connection. It wasn't her job to guide her submissive to an orgasm. The blonde existed for the seductress' pleasure, not the other way around.

"The Studio 7: The Party Favour (A Priya Story)"

written by Max D

Featuring Priya, Ash, and Max

"The Studio 7: The Party Favour (A Priya Story)" themes: FF, FFF, D/s, Femdom, Threesome, Fingering & Fisting, Vaginal & Anal Penetration, Oral Sex, Gender Transition, Exhibitionism (Couples Room, Photo, Public)

He kept to himself, seeing some familiar faces in the crowd but content to take things at his own pace, and she had to respect that. Priya had looked for Miez, for a companion, or signs of any other competition, but Max seemed to be operating completely solo at the Rumpus party. Occasional hellos were exchanged with people she didn't know or recognize, but the scene was mostly filled with Brighton regulars and token Londoners who had made the weekend journey despite plenty of alternative distractions within the city.

"The Studio 7: The Party Favour (A Priya Story)"

He would be out of his element. A funny way to think about a man who was a continent away from home, but she counted on the disruption of being in a new setting with new faces to keep him occupied until she was ready. At her side, her pet's androgyny suited the submissive's male attire, and the seductress was entertaining a handful of potential sluts while trying to determine which were best suited for her studio and personal pleasure. She could deal with Max later; business and revenue came first.

Unwittingly, he slipped out of her grasp while she was the one actually distracted. A threeway play session in the Dark Room intensified quickly when the seductress' fist popped into a darling brunette's sex while her pet lavished the woman with kisses and rude demands. Gasping and pleading for more while bucking against the hand inside of her, Priya was delighted and a few inches past the wrist when the woman's hard orgasms drenched her forearm with squirt juices. Laughing, her pet blew his insatiable Mistress a kiss before lunging forward and thrusting his tongue down the whimpering woman's throat. Unlike London, the Dark Room setting at the fetish parties in Brighton had no real boundaries, and the brunette was ravished by the demanding duo while being so firmly pushed past her limits that she had to be carried back to reality and taken to the ladies so Priya could wash her up while enjoying more one-on-one heavy petting and groping.

The sexual debauchery could have ended with that, but there were other women to conquer and men to force to kneel at her feet. Her gorgeous pet was the perfect bait and foil for hunting the party's pretty wannabes and willing servants. Each delightful taste encouraged Priya's appetite for more, and she happily dove into the deep end to submerse herself in the potent combination of music, alcohol, and sex play.

The details were a blur until moments of coherence caught up with the euphoric seductress. This time it was a pale brunette with a dyed fringe. Her petite cleavage was exposed by a swooping latex neckline that invited tender kisses. Priya adored the way she gasped and stumbled forward as her pet growled, "Do you prefer it between the cheeks or are you just for show?" His hands would be caressing the shy woman's creamy thighs, reaching up and taking the brunette's hands and guiding them under her skirt, and encouraging permission to go higher and higher until her latex circle skirt was pushed to her waist.

Moans of pleasure, of desire, and pleas for more made the seductress' pussy slick with arousal. Her rouge lips caressed the woman's neck, brushed over the edge of her jaw, and teased her pursed mouth. The moment her pet's fingers penetrated the darling, Priya was there to catch her gasp with a firm kiss. Hands holding fast to the domme's waist, the petite brunette shuddered while spreading her thighs and bucking against increasingly aggressive thrusts.

Delighted when she quickly climaxed, Priya quietly asked, "Is your tongue as ready as your pussy?" The suddenly crimson blush made her smile, and she showered the brunette with reassuring kisses while guiding her into a hug. "Don't worry. With practice. With lots of practice. It will be." The brunette was nodding, uncertain but willing, and began to tremble when wet fingers began kneading her lean buttocks. "That, too," the seductress promised. Her tongue slipped between the parted lips, seeking a response, and the pale woman exhaled into her throat while locking her knees. Breaking away, flirting with a knowing wink, Priya made her desires clear. "With practice. Lots of practice." Swallowing, the brunette's fringe stuck to the perspiration on her forehead as she tested pushing herself onto the fingers exploring the constriction of her bottom.

The three of them ended up in the toilets, and their guest's willingness to share her contact information and give Priya's drenched pussy several licks led to plans for a weekend spent doing so much more than kisses, petting, and fingering. The seductress and her pet reluctantly left the petite woman to recover, but other options presented themselves after sipping two rum and cokes while bantering with a growing gathering of regulars near the bar.

Her pet slipped away, feeling disconnected from the festivities, as Priya lured two cocks into the Dark Room. There was a strange sense of knowing what came next, of having heard all the ways that his Mistress would coax, command, and control men to get what she wanted, and not needing to see it firsthand. Any urge to protect the seductress seemed foolish. Priya was surrounded by people who would jump at a chance to prove themselves, and she preferred rough attention that was untainted with caring whenever possible. He focused on a bratty bleach blonde, guided her to his lap while plying her with compliments and questions, and enjoyed her chaste kisses and rude comments with a smile.

Priya returned, feverish and satisfied, and she immediately play acted possessive outrage before bursting into laughter. Her and the blonde bonded, comparing notes on what made the seductress' pet attractive, and taunted each other with bold dares to prove their sexual prowess. When it was clear that his Mistress wanted space to work the older woman, he left. In his absence, shared secrets would bring the women to a common understanding. There would be an exchange of information, most of it half truths, and Priya would make certain this latest conquest was theirs in trade for something so damning and perverse that the blonde would need their silence to maintain her social status. It was so familiar. It was so rehearsed and practiced and... predictable.

By the time Priya had completed the negotiation and spread her thighs to invite the older blonde under her skirt, Max had drifted off the main dance floor and into one of the side rooms. She was too satisfied by her victory, lazily enjoying the tongue lapping at her pussy as she ran her fingers through the woman's hair, to track him down. Like that, knowing she had an audience but not caring enough to bother paying attention, she was the reason Max left. Rumpus in London had always included a more sexually oriented crowd mixed with burners and latex fetish players, but the deliberate focus on sex and swinging was boring and a nuisance to avoid for a man who didn't play at parties and had no interest in naked bodies.

Random naked bodies anyway.

He stepped out, immediately struck by the darkened rat maze of Brighton's streets and pondering how to orient himself and head back toward the piers and thus the direction of his hotel without any line of sight, and paused to admire a roguish cross dressing blonde. The tells were there for anyone who wanted to see them. Slightly too lean and effeminate in the shoulders and cheekbones. Slightly too tentative while projecting a masculine stance. Slightly too body aware while pretending to feel nothing.

It was an attractive package. His interest in the unanticipated and the unusual always led him to the unstable fringe of humanity. The blonde nodded, muttered something, and he laughed.

She snapped at him without hesitation. "What?" The aggressive challenge was a dull roar in Max's ears. He could see it, the sculpting and shaping necessary to bifurcate masculine and feminine while co-existing in the same body. "You have something to say?"

Tipping his head slightly to one side, Max let his American accent speak for him. "Admiring your hard work." He immediately reassessed the circumstances as dark clouds swept across the younger woman's eyes. "Ah. Your... Mistress' work." His intuition sought out other clues. The woman presenting as a man was not collared, had no ring to signify status, but clearly was someone's pretty art project. "She must be truly amazing for you to be so devoted." He gestured with his fingers, a hat tip or a casual salute acknowledging the stranger, and went to head off in a random direction hoping it would lead him toward his destination.

"Wouldn't you like to know," the sneer made Max pause. "Not that you've got anything to show for it..."

Used to the flaccid lad culture in London, Max had already turned and coldly sized up his opponent, overtly moving his head to accompany a vertical sweep of his eyes, and grinned. "Want to start something you cannot possibly win?" He laughed when the androgynous woman accidentally took a step back. "Didn't think so. Go back to partying with the adrenaline junkies. Don't fuck with wolves who have been lured out to the middle of nowhere with false promises of a good party."

"Ha! My Mistress is a Wulf Daughter. She'd teach you a thing or two!" It came out in a rush, bravado trying to cover up fear and insecurity, but the sudden silence that followed was terrifying.

Nodding while subtly scanning the entire street for ambushes, dead reckoning shaped the emotionless tone of his voice when Max responded after long seconds had elapsed. "Oddly too specific. There are only two Wulf Daughters. I should know. I created them." His heightened awareness was conveyed by the brutal animosity of his body language. The blonde had nowhere to run, no distraction or sacrifice to hurl in his path, and perspiration beaded on her forehead as she unconsciously clenched her fists to fight the urge to escape. "So you're one of Priya's pets." He was a weapon in a land which believed there were rules of engagement. Diplomacy was an easier if less satisfying choice than throttling the island natives. "Let her know I said hello and it's nice to see that she's healthy and enjoying herself."

"And who should I say told her?" It came out as a squeak of defiance rather than the humiliating accusation that it was intended to be. Implying Max was a nobody, a non-entity, seemed impossible when facing his immensity. United by universal panic, both genders of the blonde sought a way out of the trap surrounding them.

Nodding again. Accepting this was just a fuck up of coincidences, he released his hold on the pretty party favour by simply looking away. "Max." He shrugged her off and moved on, like he always had, and never looked back as the twisting thoroughfares and pinging streetlamps swallowed him whole.

~~~

It wasn't entirely dark out, the window curtains drawn tight against the eminent dawn, as she carefully penciled Max's message onto a scrap of paper she found in the kitchen. Priya was still sleeping off the prior evening's fun, but the blonde was freshly
~~~

washed and her belongings had been gathered in a pile on the couch beside some luggage cases that she intended to claim for herself. The marks of her servitude were written on her body in obvious and subtle ways, but she no longer felt the nakedness that had haunted her whenever she wasn't wearing her heavy cock. Her feminine and masculine traits were balanced, stretch marks across her abdomen and long labia countered by bulky muscular arms and legs. Her sculpted shoulders flowed naturally into her breasts, and the straight line of her back ended in the feminine sweep of her buttocks. Androgyny had suited her best for a while, and suddenly she realized that hinted at a third path which she had never considered.

Which her Mistress had never thought was worthwhile to exploit.

Note finished with no flourish, no signature, and no goodbye, the blonde surveyed her surroundings. She had already transferred the majority of her earnings from the joint account into the personal savings she had clung to from before... well, before she discovered herself in Priya's arms. The last bit of pulling on leggings, slipping into a top and a hoodie, and then tossing her clothing and shoes into two cases was straightforward enough. She'd catch a taxi from the end of the street, avoiding waking her Mistress with the necessary phone call, and the first trains would be running soon.

Into London first. If he was still around then that's where he'd end up.

Him.

"The Studio 7: The Party Favour (A Priya Story)"

Everything she had done, all the suffering and bliss of being shaped by Priya's demented passions, had been negated by a single action. His attraction to her was undeniable. The seductress had trained her well to sense other people's interest - casual or intimate - and methodically leverage that for her purposes. He had wanted something, sought a way to fill his emptiness, and she had inadvertently been right there at his moment of indecision. No one got lost in Brighton for long at night. His hesitation, from the blonde's perspective, had been about whether he was really going to walk away instead of joining in.

Priya would have stayed. She loved basking in the debauchery and fun. She needed to be part of it, to be connected, even though the pretty domme was paralyzed by feelings of alienation. Her outrageous persona was carefully cultivated to overcome her anxiety. The submissive had watched that, understood it, and even used it to her advantage. When she needed the ultimate fuck. When she needed the adrenaline thrill. At moments like those, as she had been coached and trained, Priya's pet had no problem triggering the violent pathos which coiled within her Mistress' heart.

He didn't. He didn't even ask her name. He shot her down, never giving her a second glance, because she wasn't good enough to stick around for.

Zipping the cases shut, the blonde reflected on how that rejection would have been internalized and crippled her in the past. She studied how she reacted in the moment, old and new personalities conflicted and uncertain, as the powerful man made his peace and chose to be somewhere else. For a brief instant, she had sensed the feral snarling of his fury and icy bitterness of his still heart, and her body had responded with an intense flickering of arousal and desire which persisted even when she returned to the Rumpus party. It contaminated her. She saw the event through his eyes. The bright lights, overexuberant makeup, and half naked flirting were so very superficial, and the sweet nectar in her mouth quickly became acidic distaste. He could walk away because it meant nothing.

So could she.

Waiting on the taxi as the morning's cool air tried to grope her through her clothes, the silence was deafening. A bus passed. A few cars. Shops wouldn't open for hours on a Sunday. It didn't matter. She wasn't coming back. She was going forward.

It was easy enough to hunt him down. He didn't hide. He didn't need to use subterfuge to conceal where he went. "Lunch in London? Maybe dinner would be better? I'll make it worth your while." She added a small offering to encourage his imagination. Leaving it vague was a calculated choice. Whether Max wanted to know more about his wulf daughter's life or wanted to devour the blonde was of no real consequence. She needed an in, a way to rationalize interrupting his day, and Max wasn't known for choosing easy options anyway.

"Checking out. Funny you should email. I

presume you delivered my message."

Whatever he was thinking, the blonde needed to correct it before he woke Priya. "Left her a note. She'll sleep in late. Still enjoy wandering Southbank?" She'd paid attention to the stories. The sorts of things that Peter or Miez let slip on rare occasions when Priya's past life came to visit Brighton for a gig. A benefit of her submission was being a wallflower that no one paid close attention to, and no one thought to keep secrets from her. "My contact details. I haven't chosen where to stay tonight."

He sent her a text message, and she responded to confirm he had the right number. He probably sent an email because he had free data roaming in the United Kingdom. "I don't know you. It would be complicated to invite you to stay at the Hilton London Tower Bridge directly across from the London Bridge station." He left it at that.

His unstated challenge offered more than she could have hoped for. "I don't know you. I do know I'm very good at things you might enjoy. My taxi is here. I'll be at the train station sorting tickets shortly. London soon enough." Whatever his choice, they would play cat and mouse as long as it took for her to find a way to prove herself.

"Catch the 07:08. It's a direct to London Bridge Station. I'll be in the quiet coach. That way you can sit somewhere nearby and email me all you want without needing to speak to me." He knew his wulf daughters well enough to have a gentle laugh at their avoidant behaviours.

The taxi driver was startled by her deep masculine laugh, and the blonde waved him off while gesturing to her phone to imply the joke didn't involve him. "Your lap isn't an option? I wonder if the quiet car has someplace private. Or is that too much like her for you?" A touch of ferocity, a hint of submission, and a willingness to do anything was a powerful aphrodisiac for most men. Max would feel safer thinking that he was being underestimated.

He called her bluff. "You know better than that or you wouldn't have included a topless selfie in your first email so I knew who you were." His message was languid and flowing, and she imagined him packing up the last of his luggage and checking his backpack before surveying the hotel room for anything he forgot. "We can cut to the relevant facts. This is about you, not me. Whatever your motivation, you're operating independently or she'd be in a full blown panic. I have a place for you to stay if you want company, but I don't sleep with women I don't know." For him to continue after setting boundaries was a good sign. "I may have been a bit rough last night. Brighton is not my turf, and I should have understood what the innuendo implied instead of assuming it would a party similar to Berlin or Wien."

"I've outgrown Brighton," she replied as the cab navigated the roads.

It was a dangerous thing to say, but Max would discuss that in detail with her later after they had dropped off luggage at the Hilton and hunted down some brunch. "We all do. Doesn't mean we don't have sentimental attachments. Time changes us."

That didn't require any elaboration, and the blonde didn't comment on their perspective concerning Priya. She'd been the plaything and doll of a Wulf Daughter.

Now she wanted to know the man behind it all.

Cherish Desire Creators

Our Creators

Cherish Desire works with amazing skilled and experienced writers, editors, narrators, video narrators, models, photographers, musicians, and muses to create written, audio, and video content along with the supporting graphics, trailers, and music clips. While Max tackles the majority of assembling their contributions into a finished format, Cherish Desire would be a lot less without their involvement.

Max

Max is the go to guy for those crazy sex questions that only come up during a night of drinking. He "just knows that stuff." He also doesn't drink. So back when it was safe to go out drinking, to go out dancing, and to travel to a festival to see amazing bands and performances, he was also the one guy that was guaranteed sober. Possibly very sweaty from dancing. But sober. It was profound watching him amongst the rest of us, while we were soaring on chemicals or crashing while fighting to maintain our buzz, and he'd be going full charge. Nothing could stop him. He was unrestrainable, a stormfront of motion propelled by music, and people vacillated between being very irritated by him and coming closer to be right beside the chaos burning within his eyes. Whatever we were, however we were, Max moved orthogonally to the flow of the Zeitgeist just to prove it could be done while knowing we were watching.

That's a part of the official blurb anyway. Here's a little bit more since you've read this far.

The clubs and venues who care about their patrons and staff are closed. That doesn't mean all of them are though. We're all longing to dance so much, to go out, but with very low vaccination rates and exponential spread, the pandemic is keeping us all locked in. Everyone who can. Everyone who can survive financially. Which means far too many people have to go out, to work in person, to put themselves at risk, and to accept if they get sick then it's not like their employer or government cares. They will just get replaced by another person who needs the income as "essential workers" are treated like a disposable resource.

So we all cling to our safe alternatives. There's only so much that can be done. Remotely. Even nearby. Max comes online in a Twitch stream, waves hello, and chats with a few regulars. Not always about the stream. Not always about anything. Not always about the coming and going of great tracks. He does tend to get excited about certain bands and asks about others he's unfamiliar with. Elsewhere on social media, he posts videos and photos from streams he enjoys, along with a link so people can join him, and most of us ignore it all. Only so much that can be done, but he's subtly placing people whom he knows would benefit from a bit more support in front of his networks. Only so much that can be done, but he's doing what he always said he believed in. Directly supporting people whom he chooses to look after.

Maybe we always needed a friend like him, but he never stopped dancing long enough to know. Maybe we always got distracted by the illusions and myths he uses to keep himself safe, so we didn't know how much he was capable of. Maybe we never cared because he's always been different from all of us.

In the midst of a pandemic, I like to think some of us are recognizing that being different isn't what we thought it was. That being isolated, alienated, and excluded is what we all feel now when we can't get hugs or see friends whom we've taken for granted as Friday and Saturday night out regulars. That friends of convenience aren't friends at all when it takes an effort to reach out instead of hope for a random encounter. He's always been an outsider. He's survived all this time. Max has skillsets some of us are only beginning to discover we need. And he's using them for the good he believes in, right in front of us, without wasting time to explain unless he's asked to.

None of that would make sense. Not a word of it. Not without Twitch being such a peculiar medium where everyone can see the channel chatter at the same time in one place. Think of how many bar conversations you only hear about the day after. Think of how you have to choose to listen to the people around you or your friend right by your side. Think of how that's all flattened and visible when conversations flow and merge in a public chat stream. Most of us are still filtering, still focusing on specific people or threads, but Max doesn't have to. His divergence makes him neurologically suited to process multiple threads simultaneously. It doesn't per se work across Discord, but I know he's multi-streaming at times because he'll comment on something happening elsewhere. And his lack of concern about random strangers judging him since they always have means he also can talk freely.

All that would be fine. Unusual but totally fine. Except then he's propping up a new DJ stream, someone he also does collaborations with, and it's impossible to avoid how he subtly and not so subtly promotes and encourages others to support her. He's ok throwing money in the pot if others will join. He's cheering things on. He's that dad watching his kid play sports, getting everyone enthusiastic, and then he laughs and goes back to talking about multiple things, picking up conversations interrupted by a hype train or big tip after a moment passes, and a seemingly random set of responses to specific people flashes onto the channel. He types so fast that it's hard to tell if he's being paced by the Twitch rules. In the midst of that, he sweeps in and covers for moderators not paying attention, without ever usurping their authority, and people listen to what he has to say as if he was moderating from the start anyway.

And they haven't seen him on Zoom like I have.

They haven't seen him adjust his webcam so he can dance, all by himself, and share that with others who might feel inhibited or uncertain. They haven't listened to him casually chat with complete strangers as if he just happened to be at their local bar while traveling for work. They haven't seen how easily he blends in, asks questions about our lives, and happily chooses a plushie wolf to dance along on Zoom with our little minions for certain silly songs. They haven't seen the long goatee, closely clippered scalp, and unassuming aura of power which surrounds him in his LED backlit NOC. They haven't seen him openly admit to his crushes on certain DJs and musicians when they show up in the stream while equally showing he is completely ok with that not being relevant to anyone beyond himself much less reciprocated.

I thought that last one was a red flag. Guys always want something. And one of our leaders, far too aware of how demanding and abusive men can be, shrugged when I brought it up. "He's just being overly honest. And being really kind about it. If it makes you uncomfortable, if he says something you think is out of line, tell him. He'll fix it. As best he can." This, from someone whose pronouns he semi-regularly fucks up, was a bit of a shock. But then I realized that they get the daddy vibe from him as well. That he made it clear to them and their partner whom he knew from festivals that he knows none of us. That his interactions were frequently misunderstood. That if there are problems then he'd need feedback to best understand how to avoid friction and conflict.

I'm remembering all of this while reading Sexy Identities stories. If I had any doubts, if I didn't grasp how his ASD shapes how Max perceives and interacts with the world, then it's all here. I've been to those cosplay conventions. I've been to those eighties nights. I've been in the midst of the Dark And Loud (tm). I know those women. Those men. Or I thought I did until I saw them through Max's eyes. And that daddy vibe... fucking hell. I bet people skip right by "Sexy Identities 11: A Feline Touch." I bet they get confused over why that story is the first of "Sexy Identities Collection 2." They don't get it. Get who she is. Because it is so very clearly a story that feels out of place is what makes it so important to pay close attention. And when he emerges from his sleep, when he calls her his wulf daughter, when he refers to her as his Prince... then you know this entire story - the first of the second collection - is a reminder to Miez that he sees her power, appreciates her authority, and loves her. That they have different forms, different strengths, and that together they are even more powerful.

The sort of thing you want to hear from daddy. That you're a good girl. That he sees you. That he embraces your power. That he respects you for all the things you do. That he is happy to be with you, to stand beside you, and to hold your hand. And, at the same time, that he can do the impossible with you. Can create, literally, new moons with his strength. Yet never compares his strengths to yours. Never implies his authority makes yours less. Simply, daddy's had it, so he's gonna make some changes. Give him a minute or two, and he'll be right back.

Oh, hey, awesome daughter. Help me name this new moon I made.

Super powered daddy vibes. I wonder if Max even knows. If he understands why some women gravitate toward him. If he has any idea how many crushes that he's leaving in his wake with his shrug and wink while chatting on Zoom. Tugging his long grey and white goatee while thinking and listening hard. Making small talk with all the ladies and men. Going back to dancing. How we're watching him move like a contained explosion.

I'm going to read through these stories and try to remember he shared them without any expectations of a response. Of course, not responding is... kind of not going to work after I send him this. I'm sending it anyway. Some decisions change everything, I guess.

Maybe yours did as well.

Cherish Desire
Erotica

Very Dirty Stories

We wanted to share our favorite sex stories. The ones that broke out of the conventional erotica mold, shattered the limitations of casual romance and sex, and dove into detailed and realistic action involving stretching, large sex toy play, vaginal and anal fisting, domination, fantasy monster and animal dildo play, restraints and suspension, elaborate medical and DIY devices, and more. We did it bit by bit, discovering and learning as we went, and released volume after volume of two to five short stories to challenge readers to be sexually aroused by something truly intense or charmingly subtle. Very Dirty Stories volumes are about ladies that expose themselves and embrace their fears and desires as well as the men and women that inspire them to sexual peaks while living out wild sexual fantasies.

Singles

We wanted to publish sexual adventures that were more than a one night stand. So we gathered together our favorite ladies and delightfully sexy themes and created Singles - longer collections of sexual stories that fit together to cover formative physical and psychological experiences that define her womanhood or establish a collection of deviant delights and sexual alternatives. These trailblazing erotica books go deeper, harder, faster, and expose the soft white underbelly of sensual need while delivering thrust after thrust of sexual intensity and the soothing pleasures of passionate affection. Explore the explicit erogenous zones of women and their sexual partners. Be prepared for sexually challenging situations as well as character details that get beyond height, weight, hair colour, and favorite size of dildo. Plunge into their stories and get wet. Singles also make great gifts for that secret someone who needs a sexual swift kick in the nuts or a perverse surprise stashed for long trips and evenings in.

~~Very~~ Wicked Dirty Stories

The darkness of desires are shadows always encircling the hope of fulfillment and pleasure. These are the twisted realities fueled by the uninhibited passions and believes of the few. Their sexual urges, their powerful alliances, and their willingness to defend their own as well as to strike out and forcefully embrace what they require. ~~Very~~ Wicked Dirty Stories hint at the unobserved and strange frayed edges of reality that we like to censor or ignore. Ghosts, shapeshifters, and great powers linger just beyond the firelight while watching humanity sleep.

Divinations

Cherish Desire Divinations erotica delves into

darkness. Lusty shapeshifters, impassioned spirits, dangerous players, and perverse pagan deities beckon with sordid promises and unseemly urges. Their intense passions expose their bestial and heavenly natures while emphasizing how closely they represent unfettered hunger, cunning, love, and wickedness. Divinations was born of fevered imaginations and sexual abandonment that left us aching, bruised, and hoping for more. Divination books are collections of erotic stories that go deep and explore psycho-sexuality as well as physical modifications suited to the nearly immortal. The limited disguise of humanity has been stripped away, and the results are animalistic sexual rituals and self-enlightened spirituality that arouse jaded desires for more.

Cherish Desire apologizes in advance for exposing the true nature of shapeshifters and the transcendent hungers that lurk behind every door and under every bed.

Discover More

For our complete catalog of titles, explore our books: https://wulf.fun/CherishDesireErotica

For more about your favorite characters, check out the ladies: https://wulf.fun/CherishDesireLadies

Very Dirty Stories, ~~Very~~ Wicked Dirty Stories, Cherish Desire Singles, and Cherish Desire Divinations titles include over 450 erotica stories to delight even the most jaded readers. With a focus on perverse desires that push limits to achieve blissful pleasure, intense action and taboo desires inspire fantasies and arousal for a satisfying climax.

Cherish Desire Erotica

The majority of Cherish Desire titles are available in digital editions with audio, video narration, and paperback editions for select stories and books.

And when you visit the Cherish Desire Catalog, get elite and a free eBook from Cherish Desire by signing up for the inside track.